LIBOR MIKESKA was born in Brno, Czechoslovakia in 1967 and grew up in Australia. He studied mathematics and then languages at the University of Melbourne. He now works as a freelance columnist for the Rhein Neckar Zeitung and teaches English at Heidelberg University in Germany. He is the author of *Allegro Agitato or Neurotically Yours* and is currently working on a third novel.

Praise for the book

A lively novel which could have been entitled 'Life is a painting'. In its evolving narrative, two school friends, Sarah and Lucinda, dispersed across Old and New Worlds, explore dreams and relationships, nature and their own art. Triangular connections of families and new relationships unfold across England, the Czech Republic and Australia, in stories across time and place. The novel has a soft texture, as it delightfully fuses the imagined with the everyday. It also unravels a mystery, as the painting offers the pieces of history's – and life's – jigsaw puzzle.
Stephen Alomes (renowned author and critic)

This has everything a modern novel needs. It's an immensely involving story faithfully reflecting the challenges of finding out what really matters in life while at the same time treating its highly engaging characters with tremendous sympathy and humour.
Andrew Jenkins (translator of Alan Bennett and Alice Miller), who was kind enough to edit this book

Life's A Game You Play

Libor Mikeska

SilverWood

Published in 2017 by SilverWood Books

SilverWood Books Ltd
14 Small Street, Bristol, BS1 1DE, United Kingdom
www.silverwoodbooks.co.uk

Copyright © Libor Mikeska 2017

The right of Libor Mikeska to be identified as the author of this work has been asserted in accordance with the Copyright, Designs and Patents Act 1988 Sections 77 and 78.

All rights reserved. No part of this publication may be reproduced, stored in a retrieval system, or transmitted in any form or by any means, electronic, mechanical, photocopying, recording or otherwise, without prior permission of the copyright holder.

This is a work of fiction. Names, characters, places and incidents either are products of the author's imagination or are used fictitiously. Any resemblance to actual events or locales or persons, living or dead, is entirely coincidental.

ISBN 978-1-78132-543-8

British Library Cataloguing in Publication Data
A CIP catalogue record for this book is available from the British Library

Page design and typesetting by SilverWood Books
Printed on responsibly sourced paper

The cure for boredom is curiosity. There is no cure for curiosity
Attributed to both Ellen Parr and Dorothy Parker

One

Delete Vera?
– *beep* –
One name deleted from your address book.
Delete Xavier?
– *beep* –
One name deleted from your address book.
– *beep* –
Your address book is empty.

Lucinda had just spent an entire hour ridding her smartphone of all traces of personal information that had been stored on it. Yet just to be on the safe side, she dropped it on the ground and started to stamp on the screen with the heel of her shoe. She particularly enjoyed this part, even though she would never consider herself aggressive in any way. To her surprise the back cover suddenly came off. These things were meant to be indestructible, she thought to herself. She let out a sigh of relief and mentally deleted another item from her things-to-do-before-I-leave-the-country list.

"Good riddance!" she said, almost triumphantly, while she picked up the fragments of the broken device that didn't look as if it had a 'beep' left in it. She took one last look at the contraption that had been her constant companion for a number of years, and then hurled its remainders off the edge of the cliff. She watched the pieces fall towards the rippling waves before they disappeared without a trace to the bottom of the sea.

"Well, that's that," she said unceremoniously. She tried to focus on all the things she still had to do, such as settling a few matters at work, packing her bags and visiting her aunt, but her thoughts started to wander. As she made her way down from the cliff, her whole teaching career that spanned almost ten years appeared before her inner eyes. Perhaps I'm making the wrong decision, she thought, but refused to be consumed by her doubts. Well, it's too late to go back now, she reasoned. What am I? A boomerang! Lucinda smiled and decided that she was going to begin a new chapter in her life.

Most of us spend an enormous amount of time dwelling on the past. As we get older we start to see everything through rose-tinted spectacles, resulting in an accumulation of memories that mainly consist of the more positive episodes in our lives. Those were the days, we may sigh. Yet this is all because our brains are very skilled at pushing mundane or traumatic experiences to the very back of our minds, so that we are able to get a good night's sleep. Yet why do we spend our waking hours pondering over past fortunes or the people who have in some way made a difference to our lives? Since, however significant our memories appear to us, the act of summoning them up distracts us from the present moment, which can be just as pleasant.

Such were the thoughts that were suddenly going through Lucinda's head on this unusually overcast day in June, making her realise she had reached an age in her life when she had become aware of the passing of time.

"Whatever became of Sarah, I wonder?" Aunt Veronika broke the silence after devouring the last morsel of her scone.

It was Lucinda's last week in Exeter before setting off on her summer holidays abroad. After having seen the principal of the school regarding her sabbatical leave, she was now having tea with her favourite aunt, who lived in nearby Shaldon. They had somehow strayed into a café called *The Coffee Rush* before beginning their planned coastal walk. Lucinda always felt wiser and calmer after spending time with Veronika, so she often met up with her to discuss major decisions, dilemmas or anything else that was occupying her mind such as how time had started to take its toll on her youth and peace of mind. Yet it wasn't just Veronika's unconventional and witty insights on life that appealed to Lucinda, her aunt was also the custodian of some of the family's dark secrets, particularly one concerning her grandmother that, sooner or later, she hoped her aunt would divulge.

Lost in thoughts of the past, Lucinda was swilling what was left of her tea around her cup, when out of the blue her aunt mentioned Sarah.

"Actually, I was just thinking about her!" Then eyeing Veronika with playful suspicion, "I always said you could read minds."

"We're just tuned to the same wavelength," she answered before noticing that a black cat was staring straight at her from the window sill outside. "Oh look! Perhaps I am a witch after all." Then turning her attention to Lucinda's half-eaten scone: "Um…" her eyes widened in expectation, "if you're not going to finish the rest of that…"

"Help yourself!"

"Oh, ta!" she said gratefully, enveloping the rest of Lucinda's scone with a large dollop of clotted cream. "They're ever so good!"

While Aunt Veronika was enjoying her scone, Lucinda clutched her cup, trying to contrive a smile. Whereas most people fondly reminisced about the past, Lucinda would inwardly cringe with apprehension. She had only recently turned thirty-two and found the whole concept of time rather overwhelming. She dreaded the reality that she, too, would one day become old and start to wither away. Although she was a svelte stunner in the eyes of many, she daily scrutinized her face for any signs of ageing, often swearing that she could faintly discern the beginning of yet another latent wrinkle or a solitary strand of grey hair. I knew it would come to this – I've finally reached the beginning of the end, she would dramatise. Why on earth do we humans have to age? It is high time scientists came up with something to stop, or at the very least, slow down the ageing process. It's 2015 for God's sake! She felt they were taking their time about it, and therefore feared that she may not still be around when they finally did discover something. Her life was slipping by too quickly for her liking. Perhaps that's why she had welcomed the school's offer to take a sabbatical leave. She envied Veronika's carefree attitude towards life and hoped that her aunt's ability to age with equanimity would one day rub off on her. Well, at least long enough until advances in genetics were at a stage where she would no longer need to worry about such things, or feel obliged to restrict her diet to eating vast amounts of tofu, buckwheat and broccoli. Still, she did occasionally reward herself with a thick slice of fruit cake. Knowing that her youthful appearance was indeed ephemeral was the reason that Lucinda painted so ardently. It not only distracted her, it was an attempt to capture something in time forever.

"You and Sarah were as inseparable as twins when you were growing up," said Veronika after helping herself to yet another generous portion of clotted cream.

"Well we did share the same bench at school together for

years. We shared everything in fact, even our most intimate secrets."

"You once painted me a picture for my birthday, and then gave me two contradictory interpretations of it. I was always left in the dark with you two. I really must see if I can find it somewhere."

"That must have been over twenty years ago. It's frightening how time flies!"

"Wait till you get to be my age or as old as your grandmother for that matter. Then life really speeds up. You will at least have something to tell your future grandchildren about." Actually, she herself could tell a tale or two that would raise a few eyebrows, Veronika wanted to say but had second thoughts. "It's a shame she hardly seems to remember anything these days, yet…" she hesitated a while, "some things are better left unsaid," she concluded, avoiding Lucinda's eyes.

"What things, Aunt Veronika?" asked Lucinda intently.

"Oh, I'm afraid I can't tell you, dear. I'm sworn to eternal secrecy." She winked at Lucinda, whilst she spooned out the last of the cream and smacked her lips.

"Don't you think it's time to rid yourself of the burden of grandmother's big secret?" Lucinda insisted.

"Maybe one day," Veronika said in a rather noncommittal way.

"Oh go on! I promise I won't tell a soul!"

"When she's no longer with us. In any case, I don't know that much, probably not even the half of it. She did once promise to bequeath her diaries to me. Now, that's where you'll find all the answers! Let's just hope she hasn't lost them or thrown them out in the meantime," Veronika added before finishing her cup of tea.

"My mind boggles at what is written on those pages,"

Lucinda persisted as the cat that had previously been on the window sill suddenly jumped onto her lap. "Hey! How did you get in here then?" She started to stroke the purring creature.

"Curiosity killed the cat, my dear!" Veronika shuddered. "So be glad you don't know anything."

"Well, if the information in those diaries is as scandalous as you're insinuating, you should have them published as soon as you get your hands on them," Lucinda said while she stroked the cat, which was looking for the most comfortable position on her lap.

"You were always so curious, even when you were a little girl. I couldn't leave you out of my sight for a minute. You and Sarah were always up to something. Giggling and prattling with each other as if you both spoke your own language!" Veronika reminisced.

"Oh, we were as innocent as lambs in those days," objected Lucinda with a smile as she slung her scarf around her neck in diva-like fashion.

"Anyone would believe so, being as impeccably turned out as you both were," she began. "Oh, I do like that scarf by the way."

"Thanks! It's actually my favourite one."

"As children you both made good use of your sweet looks to conceal your mischievous nature, but once you both started secondary school, you began to flaunt your sylphlike figures. That cheeky tarting up of your school uniforms was criminal, if you ask me," Aunt Veronika quipped. Then with a grin: "I'm sure the boys were swarming over you!"

"They were all so immature back then. And not really being spoilt for choice, I even doubted whether I'd ever find a partner in the end. Sarah, on the other hand, was more optimistic, often stating that all good things took time, but then she and her parents suddenly emigrated to Australia."

"Now that was a surprise! Anyway, she could be married by now with three kids and a mortgage, for all we know."

"Sarah? Knowing her, I somehow doubt it. Still, it would be interesting to know how she's getting on," pondered Lucinda.

"How come you two didn't stay in touch?" enquired Veronika.

"We did write to each other a few times after she had left England," began Lucinda, "but unfortunately we lost all contact after a while. After all, it was in the good old days before the Internet and Facebook. Out of sight, out of mind, I guess."

"You could try googling her," suggested her aunt.

"I tried that once, but after the computer spat out a flood of *Sarah Hafner* entries, none of which were even remotely conclusive, I gave up. I suppose it's now in the lap of the gods if we'll ever meet again," concluded Lucinda as the cat jumped to the floor, eager to discover something else.

"Perhaps she has also tried googling you, since not everyone is blessed with an exotic name like yours, Miss Vánočka!"

"Don't know what's so exotic about a name meaning *Christmas cake* in Czech! I'll never understand why my father never changed his name, whereas my grandmother had to change hers for some reason."

"Your grandmother had no choice in her predicament. It was the only way she could leave Czechoslovakia back in the fifties."

"How come, Aunt Veronika?"

"Well, it was all very complicated and clandestine back then. Rumour had it that the secret service was in some way involved, so I suppose things had to be properly hushed up," she began as they got up and put on their jackets. "Something we could hardly imagine nowadays. Shall we go?" she finally said in a way that made it clear that nothing more was going to be said about the matter.

Leaving the quaint little café and heading for the shore, they looked up at the grey clouds that had gathered in the meantime.

"I see it's going to be a battle of nerves between the sun and the scudding clouds today," observed Veronika, before checking whether she had her sunglasses in her handbag or not. "Still, you've got to hand it to the sun; he's trying very hard to shine."

Her sentences often had an anthropomorphic touch to them. As the day hadn't yet been marred by rain, they decided to follow the meandering wooded path up to the craggy cliff. Overgrown branches had to be dodged every now and then, but their perseverance rewarded them with occasional glimpses of the sea.

"We could venture down to one of those coves later if you don't mind a little wind," suggested Veronika.

"It's lovely here. By the way, Veronika, I'd really like to see that painting again," Lucinda said.

"You mean the one you and Sarah gave me all those years ago?"

"Uh-huh. I'm really curious what we both daubed onto that canvas as children."

"Heaven knows where it is now, but if I ever find it I'll…"

As they continued their way, a sudden gust made it hard for Lucinda to understand what Veronika was saying. Instead of turning around, she just looked ahead and wondered whether Sarah still dreamed of becoming a famous painter one day…

Two

Beep beep beep beep – beep beep beep beep – beep... Sarah normally set two alarm clocks to prevent her from sleeping in. After turning off the first one, she treated herself to another twenty minutes of slumber before the second clock would bring any dreams she may have been having to an abrupt end...

I wonder who's going to turn up today, thought Sarah as she gazed surreptitiously around the gallery. In any case, I must try to be polite to everyone, even those malicious art critics if any bother to turn up. Sarah's friend Dorothy was late as usual. They were both being featured in an exhibition for up-and-coming young artists. Sarah loved to mingle among the guests and eavesdrop a bit before approaching them. It always proved to be rather educational.

"Look, why did you drag me along in the first place? You know that art is anathema to me. Besides, I would have preferred to go to the football!"

"Oh stop being so irritable, will you! It's raining anyway."

"No match was ever called off on account of rain," said the man, shaking his head as he obediently followed his more enthusiastic partner. "You're such a culture vulture!"

"Just try to enjoy the paintings. They're all so lovely,"

praised the woman as she headed towards another that caught her attention. "Oh, I like this one! Come and have a look…"

"Cat got your tongue?"

"No, *un ange passe*, if you'll excuse my French. Do you see what I see?"

"Oh yes, this one does ring a bell, and I'm sure the artist still remembers you!"

"It's the one the galleries were fighting over; the one that sold for almost $20,000."

"Mind you, I think it was much too high a price to demand, especially with that scathing review you gave it."

"Yeah, I tore it to bits, didn't I! Perhaps that's why it sold. They'll probably all sell like hot cakes now."

"Now, class, is everyone here? Michelle, stop fiddling with that blasted phone at once or I'll confiscate it!" warned a strict teacher who had taken his pupils to the exhibition. "Jeremy, what can you tell me about the artist's use of light in this painting?"

"Um…it's…cheerful."

"Well, that's true, but apart from the mood, she's managed to depict the bush at the brightest time of the day; it's practically pervading the whole scenery. Magnificent," he began in admiration. His voice faded as Sarah walked in the opposite direction. "Just look at that brushstroke texture…"

"Oh, there you are, my dear," began a stern-looking guest, which startled Sarah, as she almost ran into her. "Tell me, how do you explain your work to other people?"

"I don't. Um…you see, it's usually the other way around," Sarah replied with a smile.

"It's just that I've noticed that your paintings seem to

show a rather dichotomous view of the world."

"Oh really? You don't miss a thing, do you!" Sarah said flippantly, but quickly continued before the woman could react. "I guess my work just turns out that way when I dab on the paint," replied Sarah, making a mental note to look up the word *dichotomous*.

"And how do you decide what to paint in the first place?"

"Well, it's usually something that's niggling at my subconscious. Then everything just tends to unfold on canvas. It's quite therapeutic; the only problem, though, is knowing when to stop."

"I see...very interesting, um..." the woman continued, making Sarah dread another question, but a man behind them suddenly interrupted her.

"Sarah! Fancy seeing you here of all people!"

"Eric!" gasped Sarah excitedly before swiftly turning away from the woman. They embraced each other warmly. "My, it's been a while!" Sarah beamed. "What have you been doing with yourself?"

"Oh, it's a long story!"

"Then we'll have to meet up so that you can tell me all about it," insisted Sarah.

"With pleasure. Well, I can see that you haven't been wasting your time. I never knew you were such a prolific painter. I'm impressed, I must say."

"Thanks. Anyway, let me show you around. And please be honest. I want your genuine opinion."

"Well, I'm not good at lying, so brace yourself for anything," he warned her playfully.

"Should I be worried?"

"There's no need. Anyway, I've already seen most of them, and um...oh yes, there it is," Eric said, pointing to a large painting in the corner.

"I'm starting to brace myself," she said as they both made their way towards it. It was hard for her not to grin.

"Relax! I quite like this painting. It's definitely my favourite. I particularly like the way you've captured the morning light cascading through the window," said Eric eagerly, hoping his words would please her.

"Hm, I have to agree with you there. And it's not often that I see something that I wish I had painted myself," Sarah admitted in awe of her fellow painter, who had yet to arrive herself.

"You mean it's not yours?" Eric asked, quite taken aback. "Oh dear, I think I may have just put my foot in it," he said rather embarrassed.

"It's okay, really it is. I'm a big fan of Dorothy's work myself, as she's quite a talent. It's not the first time we've put on an exhibition together."

"Well, I've yet to see all the paintings, so I may change my mind," Eric said, trying to redeem his blunder.

"You don't have to just for my sake," she said unconcerned.

Amidst the yammering crowd, they walked in silence as their thoughts turned to vivid memories of the past.

"Well this is *my* favourite, if an artist is allowed to say such a thing about her own work," declared Sarah modestly.

"Very nice, and it even comes close to rivalling Dorothy's!" Eric said teasingly. "*Lucinda's dream*," he read from the title underneath the painting, before looking at Sarah enquiringly.

"I called it that on account of its surreal nature."

"Who's Lucinda by the way?" Eric asked.

"She and I grew up in England together. It's actually because of her that I became so interested in art in the first place, or rather..." began Sarah, "thanks to her eccentric grandmother, Irma. You see, she once gave us brushes and all these oil colours, and from then on we'd spend hours on end just painting as if it were the be-all and end-all to life. We even worked on paintings together, believe it or not."

"Oh, I'd love to see those!"

"So would I. God only knows where they all are now. Irma was an enigmatic woman. She wore these flamboyant outfits that seemed to belong to another era. I could somehow relate to her better than my own gran. She would never speak of her past, though," said Sarah, lost in thought.

"Big mystery, is it?"

"Indeed it is. Do you have any secrets, Eric?" she asked.

"Oh definitely; everyone has a few skeletons in the cupboard. Don't you?"

"Well apart from a couple of mouldering carcasses of art critics in my cellar…"

Eric chuckled. "Um, did your friend Lucinda also become a painter, by the way?"

"No idea. I've always wondered whether she still paints as feverishly as I do. The last time we saw each other was just before I left for Australia," she said, not without a hint of nostalgia.

"But surely you must have kept in touch?"

"In the beginning we did, but then a letter I'd written her was sent back. It was either because of a postal worker's incompetence or my bad handwriting," she said. "After that I was so overwhelmed by the avalanche of new impressions that I just forgot about her for a while," she confessed.

"Don't you ever wonder what became of her?"

Eric's question faded as Sarah slowly opened her eyes.

Three

Lucinda and her aunt continued their walk in silence. A downward thicket path suddenly opened up to a vast meadow, which then unexpectedly became a manicured golf course. They soon found themselves only metres behind two players absorbed in a game. While one player was preparing to tee off, his opponent questioned the suitability of the club he was using.

"I'd use a 5-iron for that shot if I were you, mate," advised the second golfer, crossing his arms and then playing with the onset of what looked like was going to be a beard.

"I think I'll stick to the 7-iron. It's not so far out, and it's easier to control," came his resolute reply. Lucinda and Veronika watched in suspense.

"But you've got to take the swirl of that wind into account," the second golfer continued unrelentingly.

"Thank you, Shakespeare, but I shan't heed your words, if you don't mind," the first golfer finally said, becoming tired of his unsolicited advice.

"Well, don't say I didn't warn you!" said the second golfer as his opponent struck the ball.

"Just take a look at that!"

Veronika and Lucinda began clapping.

"Thank you, ladies!" the first golfer said, and winked at them.

"How do you expect not to do well with a whirling wind like that? Okay, where's my 7-iron?"

"Told you so. Anyway, don't grudge me my moment of triumph!"

While it was the 'expert's' turn to tee off, Lucinda and Veronika's attention turned to the steep climb that awaited them. Fortunately, a welcome tailwind spurred the two upwards (yet probably didn't do much in the way of helping the second golfer, judging from the language he was suddenly using). Looking back at the golfer, Lucinda chuckled as he threw his iron to the ground in disgust.

"He'd have been better off sticking to his first choice after all," she commented.

"And I should have remembered my sunglasses!" Veronika frowned, squinting into the distance.

"In my heart of hearts I long to reach a stage in my life when I never need to use such words again."

"What words?"

"All the *should haves* and *shouldn't haves*!"

"Impossible, dear, for we all make mistakes now and then, even at my age," Veronika asserted. "Try something simpler like longing to live in a country where you don't always have to think about bringing along an umbrella and your sunglasses at the same time," she suggested.

"Okay, I'll set my heart on something more realistic," Lucinda said before stopping to catch her breath. "Climbing really takes it out of you! I read somewhere that it uses up ten calories a minute."

"Then it's a good thing we ate beforehand." Veronika felt comfortably full.

"Somehow I'm not sure that scones, jam and clotted cream are that nutritious, Auntie!" joked Lucinda.

"What do you mean? There's fibre, there are complex

carbohydrates…" retorted Veronika.

"Not forgetting the fats and sugar," objected Lucinda.

"As well as calcium, vitamins A and D. The scones were even filled with all those sultanas."

"There were only about three in each one, Aunt Veronika!"

"Anyway, it doesn't really matter what you eat as long as you use up the calories in the end."

Close to what appeared to be their first peak, they thought they could make out the sound of cows mooing. Surely enough, as they turned towards a fenced field just behind the summit, they were met by a mass of bovine eyes staring straight in their direction.

"Oh my," began Lucinda, becoming anxious, "I hope they won't charge at us or anything."

"I wouldn't worry," said Veronika, quite unruffled by the situation. "They don't look aggressive." She eyed them for a few seconds, but when she noticed that their tails and ears were flapping to keep the flies away, she decided there was no danger.

Ignoring the cows, yet keeping a safe distance, Lucinda turned around. It had occurred to her that during their whole journey they hadn't looked back once. Veronika did likewise and the most marvellous view opened up to them.

"Oh, I simply must make a sketch of the faraway sea with those undulating meadows in the foreground," said Lucinda eagerly whilst taking out a pad and a pencil from her rucksack. "You just look out for those cows. That big brown one looks as if it's approaching us," she said anxiously, as she settled on a patch of dry grass in the field.

Amidst frequent sidelong glances in the direction of the cow that looked as if it were coming closer, she began to draw. Veronika marvelled at how dexterously her niece's hand whizzed over the paper. Then she, too, sat down, taking the opportunity to relax.

"Veronika, did you by any chance see a path down to that secluded beach over there?" asked Lucinda. "We must have missed it on our way up."

"Oh that's Ness Beach. There's no access to it from the path, though." Veronika gave the impression that she was the only person who knew how to get there. "In fact, the only way down there is via the old tunnel. It's long, damp and rather spooky. The entrance is near the zoo, down past the hidden golf course we came across," she explained.

"Now I remember!" Lucinda said as further images of the past sprang to her mind. That's where Sarah and I..." She suddenly hesitated out of embarrassment.

"What, dear?" asked Veronika curiously.

"um…shared our very first kiss."

"Really? Now I am surprised! Or were you just rehearsing for the real thing?"

"Not together, Auntie! It was actually a fella called Daryl who had that privilege. Sarah fancied him or rather thought she did, and so we inveigled him to accompany us by letting him kiss us both on the lips. We were only sixteen," she avowed in all innocence.

"My, my, that was very avant-garde of you," remarked Veronika. "Still, it must have felt strange, don't you think? A bit like *Jules and Jim*, only the other way around."

"I told you we shared everything. Who are Jules and Jim by the way?"

"It's actually a cult film from the sixties, in which two men share the same woman. I saw it on my first date with a fellow student called Richard. Heavens, it seems like only yesterday!"

"How romantic! Did he try to kiss you in the cinema?"

asked Lucinda, relieved that her aunt had changed the subject.

"Well, no," she began, shaking her head, "he was so engrossed in the film, or at least he pretended to be, and much too well-behaved to even dare take my hand. Don't know why I always ended up with men who were too scared to make the first move. It must be a congenital thing," she concluded. "Anyway, we spent the rest of the evening in a nearby café arguing about indelicate liaisons."

"Oh là, là!"

"And seeing that I sympathized with the actress's laissez-faire attitude, he got worried that I might be like that, too," explained Veronika, before letting her curiosity get the better of her. "But never mind that. What about you two? Weren't either of you jealous?"

"Not really," Lucinda replied, and stopped drawing for a while. "It had more to do with the kissing rather than with Daryl, so we kind of shared him until it all lost its novelty."

"How pragmatic of you!"

"Well, it also gave us the chance to explore each others' bodies," she added.

"At that age! Now I am shocked."

"It's not what you think, Auntie," Lucinda said, shaking her head. "There was never any real sex, just lots of experimenting between the three of us," she admitted.

"My, my... Well at least there was little chance of getting pregnant."

"But, surely there must have been times when you were capricious when you were younger, Veronika," Lucinda said again in an attempt to turn the tables.

"Of course, after Richard came a host of different boyfriends, none of whom my father deemed worthy of me."

"Is that why you never got married?"

"No, I guess I was just too pernickety. What about you

and Sarah? Who ended up with that Daryl chap?"

"A girl called Kathleen whose breasts were larger than Sarah's and mine combined! And as far as I know, she actually did fall pregnant and had to take a year off school."

"Well, at least you were spared of all that fuss."

"Yeah, more or less. Anyway, we did eventually find boyfriends of our own, but they never lasted long. Most of them were too inexperienced we found. And every clumsy and disappointing attempt at anything sexual ultimately meant the end of the relationship, which was quite frustrating really. So Sarah and I usually consoled each other…" Suddenly worried that her aunt's mind might boggle unnecessarily, Sarah stopped expounding on the tribulations of her late teenage years. Then she noticed that her aunt's attention had strayed anyway. "Um, shall we make our way back down?" she suggested, "I've just finished."

"What a lovely sketch! I do envy your multi-tasking skills."

"It probably comes from teaching," Lucinda said in reflection.

"Still, it must be wonderful having such long holidays."

"Believe me, you need a prolonged holiday after teaching lively pupils!"

"Well, now you've got a whole year to recover. So tell me about your forthcoming trip. I'm ever so curious."

"Well, where shall I begin?"

Four

Lucinda pondered the quaint town from the lookout tower of the Old Town Hall. She was mesmerized by the grandeur of all the colourful buildings, the countless spires and rooftops on one hill, and then by the castle high up on another as she made her way around the viewing area. She listened to the wind while it gently played with the strands of her hair. She was happy to be able to loll away her time. As she stretched out to see the legendary crooked pinnacles of the sixteenth century Gothic portal of the main entrance, she noticed tourists thronging underneath it. She nevertheless refused to budge, immersing herself in this temporary serene splendour for a few more moments before she made her way down the tower again. Judging from the advancing clouds, she realised that a storm was imminent, yet her eyes were now focussed on the Cathedral of St Peter and Paul, overlooking the Cabbage Market. Its bells began to toll and seemed to startle Lucinda out of her idleness; they echoed audibly in the distance, following her down the steps. Everything was eerie here, she thought to herself, swearing that she had counted twelve chimes even though it was only eleven o'clock in the morning. Then she came across a four-metre stuffed crocodile hanging from the ceiling of the entrance area, which she obviously hadn't noticed upon her arrival. She had been studying it for a while, when all of a sudden the tourists she had seen came bustling towards her, armed with their cameras. No longer curious enough to read the plaque on the wall, which explained not only why the crocodile was referred to as a dragon, but why it was there in the first place, she flurried between the crowd and finally made her way out onto the busy street. She took one last look at the central pinnacle that sagged so noticeably to the left. Somehow she doubted that it really was the craftsman's revenge for not having been paid as agreed, or, as another legend goes, that he had indulged in a little too much slivovice to position it correctly. Perhaps, surmised Lucinda, the eye-catching flaw was made deliberately for future generations to speculate over for centuries to come.

Brno was the first leg of Lucinda's journey after Kamila, a Czech teacher she had met a few years ago in England, had invited Lucinda to stay with her and her partner René. Fate had brought the two together during a summer language course Lucinda had attended. Kamila, who regularly taught such courses to supplement her income, habitually asked her students why they were interested in learning Czech of all languages, and was quite intrigued to learn about Lucinda's quest for more information about her grandmother's former secret life. It so happened that Kamila had relatives in the same town where Irma had once lived. They regularly stayed in touch and Kamila even visited Lucinda in Exeter before returning to the Czech Republic to pursue a career as a translator and play the cello in a local string quintet.

Lucinda soon found herself on Freedom Square, wondering what she was going to discover next on her third day in the Czech Republic. Throughout the centre of town posters were plastered over huge pillars. One from the Moravian Gallery, featuring a black-and-white photo of half a woman's face looking upwards, caught her attention. It had such a hypnotising effect on her that she decided she simply had to see this exhibition. You never know, she thought optimistically, it may even turn out to be inspiring.

Lucinda was still surprised to hear people speaking Czech. She understood the language perfectly well, so she could make out what one bearded passer-by was saying to her as he tried to explain where the gallery in question was. In between sentences he took enthusiastic bites from his take-away pizza (she had the impression that everyone was preoccupied with eating in this town).

It had already started to rain by the time she reached the famous clock that was a popular meeting point for most people at the top end of the pedestrian zone on Česká Street, where several tram lines also conveniently met. A downpour looked as if it was only minutes away. Lucinda quickened her pace as she followed the detailed directions the hungry passer-by had given her. Two left-turns later, she found herself in an inconspicuous courtyard in front of the main entrance to the museum. The first person she saw upon entering was a bespectacled, red-cheeked woman who in many ways reminded her of her aunt back in Devon. She had been devouring a small bread roll and one paper-thin slice of salami after another before she noticed her latest customer. During her first two days here, Lucinda quickly learned that Brno was full of delicatessen shops called *Uzeniny* that sold a huge range of hams, salamis and other smoked meats, most of which had unpronounceable names such as *Křemešník*, which soon became one of her favourites. After selling her a ticket, the woman devoted herself to the rest of her lunch.

Lucinda followed the signs directing visitors to the *Czech Avant-garde Photographs of the First Republic* as if she were entering another dimension. The photographs were displayed in clockwise order around the building in many large rooms, each connected to one another by a huge doorway.

The first thing that struck her was the intricately-designed herringbone floorboards. This town was blessed with master craftsmen, she thought to herself, and hoped that one day she might have similar ones in her future home. Lucinda started to look fleetingly at each photograph as she made her way from room to room. It wasn't long before she came across the photograph that had been used for the poster to promote the exhibition. She studied it intently for several minutes: *Proč? (Why?)* by Karel Kašpařík, 1937. The surname instantly reminded Lucinda of her favourite salami. So that was the man who was responsible for such beauty. Whatever became of his model, she mused. She could have been one of his students. Had they become lovers? How old had she been at the time when war was looming. If she were still alive today, she would probably be a centenarian. She wondered how she had lived before and after being immortalised in this photo. Life is such an ephemeral picnic, and before you know it, it's over, she pondered in her usual dramatic way, wishing she could share her thoughts with someone. But the only other visitors were two rooms away, zipping through the exhibition as if their parking meter was soon going to expire. Lucinda, however, stood transfixed, this time in front of a second work by Kašpařík, depicting another ethereal beauty with her hands pressed against a window. The curtains and tulips merged with the reflection of the outside trees and raindrops. Lucinda sighed. I simply must find someone who's going to eternalise my image before my face starts to wither.

She was sure that such photographers had the ability of making their models look far prettier than they had actually been, delivering them from their insignificance, so to speak. They were the grand masters of illusion, able to bring out qualities the models probably never even knew they had, bestowing upon them enigmatic auras by the way they made them gaze, normally with slightly parted lips and faraway expressions. I also want to be remembered like that one day, she thought to herself resolutely.

The more Lucinda contemplated the tantalising photographs, the more she felt she needed to uncover their underlying secrets. Photographic perceptions of muses could only be subjective, that is, artists can only give a personal rendition of how they see their models. Photographers have the added advantage of being able to black-and-white their subjects, unveiling some intrinsic feature that would have otherwise remained unnoticed in colour. Their subconscious also seems to be able to see more than the eyes can, so subtle nuances they are probably unaware of are intuitively registered before pressing the shutter release button. Yet what kind of force guides a painter's hand when the time comes to apply the paint?

Lucinda had never been anyone's muse. The longer she thought about this, the more the idea appealed to her. But she knew she wasn't really the type of person who could blindly follow an artist's orders, for she was far too assertive and independent for that, and lacked the necessary patience. No, she concluded, the only way it would work would be if I were romantically involved with someone.

As she made her way back to the first room, she gave the *Proč?* photograph one last look, trying to imagine how a painter would have portrayed this woman. She tried to put herself in a model's shoes and wondered what it was like to be on the other side of the canvas…

Five

"Dontcha just love all those bales of hay in the meadows!" asked Sarah, glancing swiftly past Dorothy before concentrating on the winding road ahead of her. One day she and Dorothy, a fellow-student of hers, both decided to pose for each other in the countryside. On this occasion it was Dorothy's turn to sit still.

"You could have simply painted me somewhere closer to home rather than drive all this way," Dorothy complained.

"But then we wouldn't have had such a lovely setting, not to mention all those bales of hay," answered Sarah.

"Do we really need them?"

"They're nice, and besides, you can't just have an open field," replied Sarah.

"They are probably seething with spiders and bull ants," said Dorothy.

"…and hundreds of other creepy crawlies," joked Sarah.

"Eeeeh! I'm warning you, if just one bug so much as comes near my naked flesh, I'm stopping there and then!"

"I've brought some lavender oil that you can smear all over you. They can't stand the stuff."

"Well, to tell you the truth, it's not actually my favourite scent either! I'll probably get bitten and my skin will break out in a nasty rash, and then I'll have to go and see a specialist or something," Dorothy lamented.

"Don't exaggerate! You'll be all right, just put some of the oil on, so that you don't complain afterwards."

"How are you going to portray me anyway? You won't make me too fat, will you? You know that I'm usually much thinner in summer."

"No one will recognise you anyway. So stop worrying."

"Just think Photoshop, and go easy on the hips!"

I wonder if Jules Lefebvre ever had to put up with such antics from his models, thought Sarah to herself. After a long silence, Dorothy plucked up the courage to ask the question she had been meaning to ask all day.

"Have you finally seen Mr Thaunton?" she asked unexpectedly.

"What do you mean, Dorothy?" Sarah replied innocently.

"I mean out of class. Have you gone for a coffee together or anything yet?" she persisted.

Something about the way she emphasized the word *anything* troubled Sarah.

"No, we haven't," she said hesitantly. "Should we have?"

"Oh, come on, Sarah, I can tell that you like him, and you haven't exactly been subtle about it in class," she said, smiling cheekily.

"Well it's true, he is rather dishy, but I would never start something with someone who was a member of faculty," she said, trying to sound convincing.

"Well, I wouldn't blame you if you did, considering the choice of male students in our course!"

"I'm just attracted to him in a platonic kind of way. That's all," she said offhandedly. The forefinger of her left hand started tearing nervously at some loose skin next to her thumb's nail. Got to stop that horrible habit, she thought to herself. But above all, I must try and be more discreet in class.

"I could be wrong," began Dorothy to get Sarah's attention again. "But I rarely am," she concluded with a smile.

Six

"And I'd now like to focus on two female painters of the clan of artists whose works predominantly depict the unsullied ideal of the Australian bush. Interestingly enough, in Jane Sutherland's *Obstruction* we see the back of a young girl, whereas in Clara Southern's *An Old Bee Farm* the back of an older woman is visible, both are standing in knee-high grass. The young girl is surrounded by saplings and the older woman by eucalypt forests."

Sarah watched Mr Thaunton intently, her chin cupped in her hands. She was so mesmerized that she found herself struggling to keep her attention focussed on the paintings. She felt she was being absorbed by her teacher's voice, as if his words were capable of placing her under a spell that she was willingly succumbing to.

"Can I borrow a pen, please?" The spell was suddenly broken, as Dorothy's request brought her back to earth.

"Oh, sure," she replied as her hand burrowed into her pencil case in search of a blue pen.

"Here."

"Ta!"

"And don't suck on the end of it!" snapped Sarah in a whisper.

"Would I do something like that?" she asked in surprise.

"You did the last time I lent you one of my pens!"

"Did I really? Sorry, I probably wasn't aware of it; I promise I won't do it again."

"Here's Arthur Streeton's depiction of Hoddle Street in 1889," Mr Thaunton began. "As you can see, it's a far cry from the traffic-infested stretch as we know it today." He seemed to sigh. Sarah also sighed, but in an entirely different way.

"And here we have one last fine example of Charles Conder's work entitled *The Farm*. Notice his skilful use of autumnal colours and how they permeate the whole scene."

Meanwhile Dorothy, who had unknowingly started to suck on Sarah's pen, was emboldened to ask a question about the latter artist's connection to French impressionism.

"I'm sure the artist was influenced by his European contemporaries, yet it wasn't until 1890 that he left Australia for Europe. It was after all the Belle Epoque, a time when everyone seemed to be gravitating to Paris, um…" he began, but lost his train of thought once his eyes met Sarah's. "Now where were we?"

"*La Belle Epoque*, Mr Thaunton," said Sarah dreamily, making her eyes appear larger for a fraction of a second.

"Oh, yes…of course. Okay, now I'd like to take a look at a few painters who were in some way influenced by the Heidelberg School. If we just consider characteristic features of individual works, the artist Lilith Leach immediately comes to mind. Although relatively unknown, her early works surely deserve more exposure. *Contemplation* is a quintessential example. No matter how much we may be in awe of her depiction of the model's beauty as she gazes at the crushing waves below the cliff tops…" he paused. As he faced the class, his eyes met Sarah's and once again he lost his train of thought. Sarah then deliberately averted her eyes, and suddenly looked disapprovingly at Dorothy.

"Stop sucking on my pen!"

"Sorry! It's become a bit chronic, I'm afraid," she said apologetically.

"Um…in her series of paintings from 1901 entitled *The Chasms of Love*," Mr Thaunton continued, "we soon become uncomfortably aware of the model's disenchantment, which can only be described as forlorn."

Having stopped frowning at Dorothy, Sarah turned her attention to Mr Thaunton's lecture.

"It evokes the sense of bitterness she felt on account of her lover's unresponsive demeanour. This, of course, was due to the realisation that his heart longed for something other than her love and devotion. He appears to have long detached himself from her influence and is aspiring to new horizons. Parallels have often been drawn to the phantasmagorical events in Kafka's unfinished novel *In search of the missing reason*. The time the artist had spent in Europe was actually a learning process and had paradoxically brought her closer to Australia. *I advise only the hardiest of painters to seek inspiration in the Old World*, warned the artist in her letters from around the turn of the century. *There is much to learn here and you'll be a better painter for it, but make sure you can sell enough of your work to pay your board and heating; and should you be among the fortunate ones, beware the lure of the temptations of the night, as many here have succumbed to a wretched incurable malady, and shan't be returning home*," concluded Mr Thaunton. "Well that's all we have time for today unfortunately," he said after taking a quick look at his watch. "Next week, I'll try to end on a more light-hearted note, but perhaps you can help me by describing a painting that has left a positive impression on you." Suddenly he noticed that Sarah's eyes were fixed on his. "Or one that has aroused some kind of emotional response…"

Seven

Sarah's head was still reeling from the realisation that she and her teacher had actually been flirting during not only the last lesson, but when she came to think of it, most of the classes she had attended that semester. Yet the closest they had got to one another was the time they happened to meet on a tram going up Swanston Street towards the University, both late for class. It was a beastly Melbourne morning in the middle of May. They didn't realise that they had been on the same tram until they were greeted by a sudden torrential downpour as they were getting off. Despite having shared Sarah's umbrella – how useful of her to have remembered to pack it in her huge handbag that morning – they both entered the seminar room rather soaked. The flustered pair whose cheeks were visibly flushed must have appeared quite a sight to the rest of the waiting students sitting peacefully in rows. Yet if that coincidence and all the other fleeting moments were anything to go by, thought Sarah, well, anything could happen, couldn't it? She was able to dispel any ambiguous feelings every time she noticed certain things such as subtle changes in Mr Thaunton's voice when he spoke to her; his eyes would widen slightly, and the otherwise eloquent academic was at a loss for words as soon as it dawned on him that she had been looking at him with that alluring smile of hers. My presence is starting to trouble him in front of his own students, Sarah surmised. As surges of adrenalin streamed through her in class, she would sigh but tried her best not to give herself away, as she knew there was some unwritten law on student-teacher conduct that forbade such a thing. She wondered how many other students apart from Dorothy had noticed anything – possibly that horrible attention-seeking Tracy, judging from the condescending expression on her face. I don't know why she always has to roll her eyes with contempt every time she looks at me. Of course, *she's* God's gift to the earth, isn't she! Always flaunting her knowledge and asking erudite questions. Releasing some of those pent-up tensions would do her a world of good. Still, she probably doesn't have regular sex, if she has any at all! God, why am I being so bitchy? She's probably just envious of Mr Thaunton's attention towards me.

In any case Sarah was determined to get to know her admirer better. If only we could be having a nice tête-à-tête at a faraway café where neither of us could be recognised by anyone, Sarah wished. She imagined the two of them sitting at a small table and stirring their cappuccinos. Only then would we really be at ease. Speculation about such things not only got the better of her at times, it also proved to be quite dangerous. One day, walking along Faraday Street from an extended lunch break back towards the campus, she was so lost in thought that she almost got run over by a tram. The sudden insistent clanging of the tram's bell brought her back to reality and undoubtedly saved her life. This teaches me once again, she silently reprimanded herself, how potentially fatal love can be. Anyway, perhaps I should just forget about him. He probably has a girlfriend or a wife and a couple of prissy kids at home in some dreadful middle-class suburb. Still, he never wears a ring, so maybe there's hope after all! Get real, Sarah, she would tell herself. What would he see in me? I am a mere student of his, one of many, but then again, being an older student, I'm probably not *that* much younger than he is. Come to think of it, I wonder how old he really is, thought Sarah. Forty? Forty-five? For all I know he could be thirty-three like me, but somehow I doubt it, judging from the wrinkles around his eyes. Or perhaps he's a lecherous lecturer who…oh, come off it! Why do I always have to think so much?

What was Sarah supposed to do? She couldn't simply brush off the emotions that were germinating deep within her. Between classes, during lunch and on her way to and from university, her thoughts were wreaking havoc on her sensitive mind: Am I going to abide by other people's *shoulds* and *shouldn'ts* and let them make my decisions for me? Why do I worry about what Dorothy or the others might think of me? Do I really need their approval? It's not my life's mission to please my fellow human beings by making sure I never do anything that might contradict their view of the world. Why can't I just ignore my judges? After all, I don't subscribe to their arbitrary rules on morality, do I! If only I weren't so vulnerable. Perhaps I could take some valerian drops or something homeopathic that will erase all my anxieties and disheartening thoughts. Have to find something to distract myself; that always helps. But, more importantly, which famous painter am I going to analyse for homework?

If only Sarah had someone like Lucinda to whom she could express her innermost thoughts, yet the friends that she had made since coming to Australia had all gone their separate ways, either commencing their studies at other universities, pursuing careers, starting families or even going abroad. She herself had already completed one degree, and spent seven years teaching at a secondary school before taking a year off (much to her parents' anguish) to simply paint to her heart's content. Not only did she feel that that year was the most satisfying in her life, she finally had enough paintings to put on her own exhibition. Now as a student again, she tended to withdraw into her own little world made up of her painting, her neurotic thoughts and romantic ideals, which she projected onto Mr Thaunton, believing he in some way held the key to her inner peace. Being much younger than she was, neither Dorothy nor any of her university friends could reassure her, so there wasn't really anyone she could confide in. I ought to just be myself, she reflected. From now on, I'm going to be more assertive and stop being such a galah. Anyhow, I'm old enough to know better.

In that solitary world of hers, memories of the past, in particular her childhood in England often surfaced and danced before her eyes. Lucinda often popped into her mind, but they had long been out of touch, which made her wonder what direction her old friend's life was taking...

Eight

"Just go down the steps here, through the underpass," explained a friendly passer-by. "Watch out for pickpockets, though; the place is seething with them! Follow the stalls, then turn left and it's straight ahead."

"Down through here," Lucinda repeated, hoping not to forget all the details. "Along the stalls, um…" she hesitated.

"Keep left until you see the large Vaňkovka sign," he reiterated.

"Thanks!"

"And keep an eye on your handbag!" he warned her again.

Still time to buy some postcards, thought Lucinda as she strolled towards the enormous shopping mall. Shoppers always seemed to be in a rush here, and the place was teeming with them. In general, she found that people in Brno were either friendly or rude, depending on which part of the city you happened to be in. It seemed to her that the closer you were to Česká Street, the more relaxed and helpful people appeared to be, whereas further down towards the main station, she felt agitated and alert as if something unpleasant was about to happen. *'Why can't you look where you're going, you ox!'* was not even the worst thing that she heard people say to each other as they scurried to and fro about their business. Yet *vole*, the Czech word for ox was something that

Czechs, especially youths, liked to call each other for some obscure reason.

Having had enough of the mall, she decided it was time to head back. Surprisingly, she made her way through the throng with ease and was only insulted once. There must be an invisible border somewhere around here which affects people's moods and their patience, she concluded halfway along Masaryk Avenue.

High time for an ice cream, Lucinda told herself as she walked across town and up towards St Jacob's Square in search of the café Kamila had recommended. The two were to meet there during Kamila's lunch break. It was off a street called *Kozí*, which made Lucinda laugh, as she had just been called a *stupid goat* herself by a cantankerous old man for apparently not looking where she was going. She suddenly thought of England and how polite and friendly people were compared with a large number of this Slavic lot. She now stood in front of the street sign and wondered if its name meant *goat's street* or *goatish* or perhaps there had once been a goat market nearby. She soon discovered people sitting outside under parasols, some devouring large bowls of ice cream, others sipping coffee. That must be the café, she assumed, and made her way with a springy step towards the only free table near the entrance. Seeing that Kamila hadn't arrived yet, she took out a pen and a postcard depicting the crooked spires of the old town hall from her handbag and began to write.

Brno, 20th July 2015

Dear Aunt Veronika. Greetings from Brno! I've only been here a few weeks, but I think I could really get used to living in this town. I've made some lovely new friends and even found a job waitressing in a café whose interior looks like Gran's old living room. I think you'd also love it here – although they don't have scones, their sweet pastries more than make up for it! Oh and thanks for sending me the contact details of your cousin Klara and Irma's sister, who live way out Woop Woop in the Moravian countryside. I have already written to them and am awaiting their reply.

Hope you're well and enjoying the English summer.
Love, Lucinda

Perhaps that cousin of mum's and Veronika's knows more about Irma than anyone back home does or is willing to reveal, she mused. Irma's sister Milena should in any case, provided the sands of time haven't buried all her memories. Kamila's a bit late, isn't she? I'm sure I got the right place, though. Before Lucinda could speculate any further, quick footsteps could be heard approaching amidst the din of the bustling town.

"Hi, Lucinda, sorry I couldn't get away any earlier. Been waiting long?"

"Not at all, I used the time to write my first postcard," she said as Kamila took off her jacket.

"What have you been doing all day?" she enquired.

"Oh, just shopping and getting used to Czech etiquette," she said diplomatically.

"People can be quite rude here," Kamila said. "Oh, before I forget, this letter came for you today," she said, handing it over to Lucinda.

"Thanks," she replied, before opening the letter. "Hey, I've been expecting this; it's from my relatives," she said, and began to read.

Luhačovice, 19th July 2015

Dear Lucinda,

Thank you for your letter. Your aunt Veronika also wrote to me a while back informing me that you were spending some time in the Czech Republic and keen to visit your relatives while you're here. You are most welcome to come and visit us. If you feel like seeing the magnificent countryside up here, you can visit me any weekend in Luhačovice, as I work during the week, but it's quite a way; probably a two-hour bus trip. Otherwise we could all meet at my mother's house in Podbřežice, which isn't so far away from Brno. Ring me anytime in the evenings on 5717359162.

Looking forward to meeting you soon.
Your Aunt Klara

Perhaps now I'll learn some intriguing things about Irma's past, thought Lucinda to herself as she finished reading. Yet even if Veronika and Klara only have an inkling of what Irma had been up to all those years ago, surely Milena must know more than anyone else does. Maybe I should visit them separately, she speculated.

"Where's Pod-bře-ži-ce and a place called Luha-čo-vi-ce by the way?" asked Lucinda, not without some difficulty in pronouncing the names.

"I know Podbřežice quite well, as one of my uncles lives there," Kamila began. "It's about half an hour's drive from here, and actually not far from the very battlefield where Napoleon had one of his greatest victories," she lectured.

"There must be quite a few ghosts in that place, I imagine."

"I doubt if there are any still lurking after two hundred years, though," said Kamila reassuringly, "and the other place is further east towards the Slovakian border."

"I'll start with the first unpronounceable place," she said resolutely.

"When are you thinking of going?"

"Well, I'll have to ring Klara first to arrange a time. Hmm... I know, perhaps I could go and see Milena this Friday after my early shift. I'll stay the whole weekend if she'll have me, although I've never even met these people before," Lucinda added, a bit uncertain. "I only know them from photographs and Christmas cards."

"You needn't worry about that, people from the Moravian countryside are extremely hospitable. If you're one of their ilk, they'll be cooking, baking and making sure you're as comfortable as possible."

"Do you think they'll let me in on some family secrets?"

"Not if they're murky ones, they won't, but they're likely to tell you all sorts of funny anecdotes about themselves and all your unknown relatives. Oh, and beware, they love to drink slivovice and eat hearty meals. Even several times a day!"

"How am I going to cope?" Lucinda sounded worried.

"Just don't get invited anywhere more than once on the same day, otherwise you'll get fed whether you have eaten or not," Kamila warned. "And don't be surprised if they serve you goulash or thick sausages for breakfast."

"That doesn't really sound like my diet somehow," declared Lucinda as she thought about her strict adherence to well-balanced and frugal eating rituals. "But my aunt Veronika would feel right at home, I can tell you that," she added.

Kamila's knowledge of Moravian villages, customs, traditions and people with astoundingly healthy appetites was going to come in handy, Lucinda realised.

At that moment a waitress appeared and handed them the menu. Feeling overwhelmed by all the choices, Lucinda and Kamila both ordered what a couple at a neighbouring table were eating: chocolate ice cream with fresh cherries.

"Oh, before I forget, has Pavel contacted you yet about giving some English classes?" asked Kamila.

"He has, but it wasn't a teacher he was after. He asked me to join his jazz band of all things!" she replied.

"He what? You must have impressed him with your deep voice. Although, I thought they already had a singer."

"They do, but she's currently pregnant and is understandably going to take some time off," Lucinda explained.

"Oh, I see, so you'd just be replacing her. Well, are you going to consider it?"

"I'm tempted, especially because he likened my voice to the singer of that Dutch band Shocking Blue from the sixties. Though I'm supposed to be on sabbatical leave, you know, taking time off to relax, paint and find out something about my grandmother's mysterious exploits…"

"Yeah, I guess you're right, but it may turn out to be fun," Kamila said encouragingly.

"True, but I told him I'd have to think about it, seeing that I'm not very good at remembering lyrics," Lucinda admitted.

"You never know, it may work out," Kamila said optimistically.

"Well, only until they find out that I can't actually sing at all!" she said apprehensively.

"Oh, before I forget, there's a flat on Jiráskova Street that's going to be free next month. One of René's colleagues is getting married and will be moving into a bigger place with his wife-to-be."

"And they'll soon be needing room for their children-to-be, I presume."

"Exactly. Well, that's the way the cookie crumbles in this country. Anyway, you're quite welcome to stay with us, but you'll definitely have more privacy there."

"Look, that's terribly kind of you and René, but you've had to put up with me long enough, so I think I should check this place out," Lucinda said, very determined.

"It's only three tram stops away from our flat, so we won't be far from each other. What more can I say, um…it's nice and cosy, apparently half-furnished and affordable," Kamila concluded.

"Sounds ideal. When can I see it?" Lucinda asked eagerly.

"I'll try to arrange a date for you once you're back from Podbřežice."

"Brilliant. Everyone's so organised in this country, it's great."

"I think enthusiastically pragmatic would be a more appropriate term," Kamila said in reflection.

"Well, as long as it works," said Lucinda practically. "Where I come from, most people love putting things off."

"What are your plans for the rest of the afternoon?" enquired Kamila.

"Recovering from this eventful day and turning in early, for I have to get up with the birds tomorrow," grumbled Lucinda.

Nine

The alarm clock suddenly went off. Sarah let it ring for a while before turning it off. Just a few more minutes, she thought to herself as she turned away from the contraption that abruptly put an end to her sleep every morning. She cuddled up to her pillow and drifted into another world…

Eric had already been awake for some time. He and Sarah had spent a predominantly restless night due to the swelteringly hot spell of weather they'd been having over the past week. The moon was also full, something that Sarah dreaded every month. She got up reluctantly and opened the curtains.

"Oh please, no more sunshine!" she complained, glaring into the distance.

"What a glorious morning!" announced Eric more cheerfully as he got up. He stretched and yawned, still thinking about the blissful night they had spent together. Sarah on the other hand had difficulty focussing on moments that simply didn't 'exist' any more, no matter how pleasurable they may have been.

Seeing that the long-awaited cool change still hadn't arrived, despite the weather girl's continual reassurance that it was fast approaching, they decided to forgo their habitual long-drawn-out Saturday breakfast, and drive as far as they could along the west coast instead. In any case, they were both itching for a brief change of scenery.

A myriad of breathtaking coastal views and about two hundred kilometres later, neither Sarah nor Eric could take any more of the serpentine country roads, so they parked their car near the next lookout point, got out and just stood there and breathed. It felt exhilarating. A sign designating the *Loch Ard Gorge* of the Port Campbell National Park welcomed them. They followed the path until they reached the wooden steps that had been erected on one side of the cliffs to enable people to get to the shore.

"How practical. I was wondering how we were going to clamber down to the beach," Eric called out to Sarah, who was lagging behind. He was just about to descend when he turned around to notice that Sarah had veered off the path through the daisy bushes that thrived all around.

"It says here on this plaque that the *Loch Ard* was a ship that ran aground on Muttonbird Island in 1878 not far from this very spot," she read aloud.

"And I thought that Loch thing was just another sea monster," said Eric, who couldn't help but laugh.

"Of the fifty-four people on board the English vessel bound for Melbourne, there were only two sole survivors called Eva and Tom. Imagine that!" she continued, becoming increasingly captivated by the history of the place. "Actually it wasn't the only shipwreck. Four other ships had met a similar fate sometime in the nineteenth century."

"The gods obviously weren't happy about the newcomers from the Old World."

As they walked towards the top of the treacherous cliff, the wind lunged at them unremittingly as if trying to prevent them from coming any closer. Eric suddenly stood still, sensing the danger, but Sarah went on further to about two metres from the edge and just stared ahead. She took off her glasses that had become blurred, closed her eyes and enjoyed the invigorating feeling of the sea spray. She stood there motionless. Whilst Eric was still considering what it must have felt like for the two survivors after having escaped death almost a hundred and forty years ago, Sarah was lost in thought, hurling wishes at the rumbling sea below. It wasn't as if she felt any foolish need to defy the elements or scare herself silly, it was just that there was some force that seemed to be summoning her closer to the edge. She suddenly got down on her knees and lay down on her stomach; then with the help of her elbows she moved as close to the edge as she could, sticking out her neck like a turtle. Poking her head over the cliff, she became quite giddy watching the crashing waves below. Enough thrills for the time being; now all I have to do is find a way to get back safely, she thought to herself. Sarah felt like a lizard as she scrambled away from the cliff's edge.

Careering from side to side, they both started to make their unsteady way down the wooden steps. Despite the fury of the wind, Eric's short hair seemed only slightly ruffled compared with Sarah's long strands that were fluttering in all directions. Above them, seagulls let themselves be carried away by the wind's force.

"And I thought Melbourne was windy!" shouted Eric.

"No, this place wins hands down," agreed Sarah, slowly starting to get used to the strong gale.

They both trudged along the wide shore as if they were climbing a steep hill, such was the force of the rugged elements. Not only was walking a strenuous task, the waves and the roar of the wind grew to stifling dimensions, making communication all the more difficult. But since neither Eric nor Sarah was particularly keen on saying anything, they walked on in silence, absorbing the unspoiled scenery.

Sarah wondered why they had so little to say to each

other. Their relationship was, after all, exactly what she had kept in her thoughts all these years, her ardent wish fulfilled at last. Had she possibly left something out? Is this what all couples go through after spending a certain amount of time together? Then marry before they run out of things to say to each other? And if that time came, was pregnancy meant to be the next inevitable step? A mere distraction from the fact that there was nothing more to say than the predictable? What else did she need for fulfilment? What was life about anyway? Painting? Work? The goals we try so hard to reach? What keeps us going? Our daily rituals? She sighed. Life was much simpler in the past: full of expectations, a whole new world to discover, yearning for another reality…

"Eric, where are you going?" she began anxiously. "Don't go too near the water's edge; you don't want to end up being carried out to sea. You know how unpredictable the tides can be," she said before turning in the opposite direction. She had only walked on for a few minutes, when she stumbled on some thick ropes that the sea must have brought in not long ago. "Look what I've found, Eric!" she said aloud, but when she turned around there was no one in sight. "Eric?" she said, biting her lip. "Where are you? Eric!" she screamed, and started to panic. "Eric! Eric…" She suddenly realised that she was alone on the vast expanse of sand.

Sarah gave up trying to fall asleep again, as her heart was beating vigorously. She began ruminating over her dream or the dwindling fragments of it that made any sense to her at all.

That's it! Sarah thought aloud. We're only ever happy when we're striving to attain something we haven't already got! It's the whole mystery about the unknown that keeps us craving it, yet as soon as we have achieved something, we have reached the end…

Ten

This is probably a wild-goose chase, thought Lucinda as the old bus plodded along the winding roads of the Moravian countryside. In any case, it was nice of Milena to invite me at such short notice; she sounds really adorable. I'll probably come back three kilos heavier, though! The views are lovely, she sighed, soaking up the splendour of the snowy plains. My great-aunt will probably wonder why I'm so keen on finding out so much about her sister, Lucinda pondered as she removed a second pullover. The heating system under the seat was quite effective, and she now had several layers of clothing piled up on her lap. A girl sitting in the aisle seat next to her occasionally gave her a shy look when she managed to tear her attention away from her smartphone. She's only about ten, thought Lucinda and she's already hooked on the cyber world. Her mother was busy tending to her younger brother, who was constantly making a fuss. Lucinda was transported into another world, completely unlike her own. She tried hard to imagine where she would be now if she had grown up in this country. Maybe like all the young mothers around her who seemed to be preoccupied with their children, the be-all and end-all to their existence, she thought. This made her wonder what it would be like to constantly be at the service of a helpless toddler or two: the sleepless nights, changing nappies, the dreadful screaming. A baby suddenly burst into tears, letting out a shrill cry. All these kids being fed sandwiches and biscuits made Lucinda hungry, so she took out her packed lunch and started eating. No, motherhood was definitely on hold for the time being, she thought as they passed the very battlefield where Napoleon's army had the most glorious of victories in 1805. She had just overheard one bright child proudly telling his mother this historical fact as if he were one of a cherished few who knew this. Well, at least they're all clever here. In comparison, I hardly know anything about British history. Perhaps my baby will be a gifted genius, she contemplated. She knew only too well, however, that such speculation was purely hypothetical. Having finished her food, she yawned and focussed her attention on the enchanting countryside again. Well, whether you end up with a quiet angel or a boisterous monster, it still needs to be taken care of. I just hope my hormones grant me a few more years before brainwashing me into parenthood. The rhythmical movements of the bus were slowly beginning to lull her to sleep.

"They're exquisite, they really are, but I don't think I could manage another one," said Lucinda while she savoured her fifth fruit dumpling. There goes my diet! She frowned as she thought about all the rich food she had become used to eating during her time in the Czech Republic.

"I'm glad you like them. Would you care for some more cream cheese?" asked the woman who had been feeding her child.

"Maybe just a small spoonful, please."

The woman served her. At that moment three more fruit dumplings fell onto her plate out of nowhere. She started to push them aside, yet five more plonked simultaneously into the cream cheese, which splattered her face. After she had wiped her eyes clean, she opened them to find her plate had broken under the weight of all the dumplings which had accumulated. Most were filled with plum jam or apricots, and had opened under the pressure of all the new ones landing mysteriously on top of them. They had also grown in size and the filling was spurting out in all directions. Lucinda was suddenly surrounded by enormous fruit dumplings. At first it felt pleasurable, but soon they began to suffocate her. The whole bus was filling up, yet just as the dumplings reached her neck, all movement stopped. Well, at least I can still breathe, she thought, counting her blessings. She then felt something fall onto her hair, her nose and even her eye lashes, which began to flutter nervously. It took her a while to realise that it had actually started to rain poppy seeds. First they were pelting her from all directions, but they soon formed into thick black blobs mixed with sugar and melted butter – to be able to breathe Lucinda had to eat as much of the advancing food as she could…

The bus jolted to a halt on the main street of a small, quaint town. Suddenly awake, Lucinda opened her eyes abruptly and quickly put on every item of clothing that she had taken off. Her heart was still racing. She got off the bus to find that the driver had already unloaded her small suitcase. After thanking him, she noticed an elderly lady approaching who immediately reminded her of Irma.

"You must be Lucinda!" the woman said cheerfully.

"Milena! I'm so glad to meet you," she said, putting her arms around the woman who looked like a younger version of her grandmother.

"Did you have a nice trip, dear," she asked.

"Lovely, thanks. I fell asleep near Slavkov and started dreaming about fruit dumplings, of all things," she said nervously.

"Dumplings?" said Milena, leading her towards the house. "I'm sure you must be hungry then. I've made us some lunch. You're not a vegetarian, are you?"

She shook her head and started to mentally prepare her stomach for a hard slog.

Eleven

"What was it like growing up with Irma?" Lucinda asked, not wishing to disclose that her grandmother had been categorically evasive about her life in Czechoslovakia.

"Well, what can I tell you that she hasn't already told you herself, dear?"

"She's very secretive at times, and mum thinks she has forgotten quite a lot," explained Lucinda. "And as for me, I feel as though I don't know anything at all about our family past, especially on my mother's side."

"Being as talkative as Irma, you'd think she'd have told you a tale or two! Would you like another piece of cake, Lucinda?"

"You're very kind, but I couldn't eat another slice, especially after such a hearty lunch."

"You should eat more, girl; you're practically skin and bones. Irma was the same when she was younger. Mind you, we were both good eaters in our youth, which was probably normal for anyone living on a farm. Yet I wasn't so lucky around the waist," she said in self irony. "Luckily we always had enough to eat. We had hectares of land to grow our own potatoes, carrots and lots of other vegetables. We had chickens, pigs and also fruit trees as far as the eye could see."

"It sounds ideal."

"It was a lot of hard work, too, and our parents were good people, for they gave work to anyone unemployed in the village. We had to get up with the birds, but all in all we had a very loving childhood. Very different to the upbringing kids have these days."

"You're right there, all you ever see are young people hunched over their phones."

"I'm sure it can't be doing their eyesight any good, and lots of them even have allergies and other disorders. We never had any of that; neither did you, come to think of it. Your generation must have been the last to enjoy growing up normally. Irma used to write to us saying how you were turning into a clever girl, and she even taught you how to paint, I heard. I still have all her letters," Milena added nostalgically.

"What were your school years like, Milena?"

"Fine in the beginning, but then practically all our teenage years coincided with the war, so it wasn't very cheerful around here."

"Neither was what followed, I imagine."

"We had all hoped things would simply return to how they had been before the war, thinking we would all prosper again, yet we ended up on the wrong side of Europe and suffered the consequences for over forty years. But that's nothing new to your ears."

"Thank God, it's over now. Did you expect it to last so long?"

"Actually, we thought it would never end, to tell you the truth. Of course, we were overjoyed when the nightmare was finally over, but they left so much irreversible damage, dear. It'll take generations to mend all that. It's only been, what, twenty-six years since the history books changed again, and there's still a lot of work to be done. It even took them a while to give us some of our property back. You know that they virtually took everything away from us back in the early fifties, don't you?"

"Gran did mention something about it having to turn into some agricultural cooperative against your wishes."

"Against everyone's wishes, dear! No one was asked. They were just informed that their properties were to come under state control, and be absorbed into what became known as compulsory collectivization for all, like it or not," she began.

"I suppose those who had nothing and opportunists trimming their sails to the wind were all in favour."

"Yes, there were plenty of them around," confirmed Milena.

"But hadn't you seen it all coming?"

"We were still recovering from the shocking news of the Communist coup in 1948, thinking it was all a bad joke. Yet, since history had taught us that we couldn't rely on the West any more, we just had to grin and bear in," she said, looking out of the window as her dog started to bark. "But as you know, Irma didn't take things lying down, and had a few less than flattering things to say to the party official who came to take away everything we owned," she concluded, still looking out of the window.

"Well she has calmed down a lot, although it's true that Gran was never one to mince her words," Lucinda said.

Milena opened the window wide. "Stop barking, Bobík!" Then turning back to Lucinda, "I still think having to spend a year in prison was a high price to pay for her indiscretion, though," she said, and then went to the window again, as the dog continued to bark. "Bobík, stop it, it's only little Gabriela and Jitulka playing. Come here and I'll give you a biscuit, that's a good boy," she called out, and made her way to the door.

Mouth agape, Lucinda had just discovered one of Irma's

secrets. What could she have said to land her such a severe sentence? Well, thought Lucinda, probably something against communist ideology, for they didn't take kindly to anyone with a defiant attitude. Or maybe she turned violent and started to beat him or attack him with a sickle. That would have given him a taste of his own medicine. Yet it was highly unlikely, seeing that Irma wouldn't hurt a fly. Before Lucinda could ponder any further, Milena had entered the kitchen once again and was just about to make herself another cup of tea.

"What exactly did Irma say to the official, Milena?" Lucinda asked eagerly.

"Oh it was something like: 'You wretched communist villains are all going to be hanged by the balls on the nearest branches when your reign is over!' or words to that effect. I can still see the stunned expression on that man's face as if it were yesterday," Milena began. "I think his name was Jaroslav Tučnák or it could have been Bohuslav, for all I know. Well, in any case, he just stood there speechless while I couldn't help bursting out in laughter. Most of them weren't very intelligent, you see, and he was no exception. The last thing you should do to that mob, however, is to offend or laugh at them," she added. "I was lucky I wasn't arrested myself, come to think of it."

Lucinda couldn't hold back her laughter either.

"She was witty, alright. But believe me, there was nothing to laugh about in those days, dear!"

Remarks that would probably be shrugged off as innocuous in today's terms were not appreciated after the communist takeover of Czechoslovakia. Yet Irma wasn't the only one who had difficulty minding her tongue, and so, just like her, many others soon found themselves behind bars with other 'counter-revolutionary imperialist intellectuals' who had turned out to be equally uncooperative with the authorities. In her case, it was in a prison on the outskirts of Zlín renamed Gottwaldov after the then president.

Up till then, Podbřežice had been spared the ongoing process of repressive nationalisation affecting every company, factory, institution, residence or farm. But it was by no means forgotten. The communist party was ruthless in its bid to eradicate any notions of private ownership and any memory of the freedoms enjoyed in the First Republic, freedoms ingrained into the fabric of the liberal-minded Czech psyche.

Milena's brother Tom was immediately told to leave the conservatoire, where he had been studying brass instruments and organ for well over five years and was even ready to take his final exams. This didn't particularly interest the new government, so he was given a new direction in life. Agriculture or mining were the only fields left open to him in the government's ideologically motivated campaign to proletarianize the bourgeoisie. Tom was fortunate that they hadn't sent him to work in the mines, but he could hardly muster any enthusiasm for agriculture. On a positive note, they did eventually let him play the organ at village funerals. But whatever they did, whether it was forcing ex-managers to drive trams, turning lawyers into electricians or subjecting academics and dissidents to back-breaking work in the mines, it was hardly a step closer to harmony, stability and equal division of wealth. They did however manage to single-handedly send the country into galloping economic ruin, not to mention devastating the agricultural industry that had been thriving before the war.

"I wonder what it must have been like for Irma in jail," Lucinda said in the hope of finding out more from her loquacious great-aunt.

"You mean, she never told you anything? Not even later on?" asked Milena in bewilderment.

"Not a word, at least not to me. Aunt Veronika must have known something, but whatever she knew, she kept it all to herself," Lucinda told her astonished great aunt.

"Well, I guess," Milena speculated, "it's not exactly something people usually boast about, is it?"

"What was she like when she came out?"

"I'll never forget the day she came home and told us all about it. But it's such a long story. Let's talk about it tomorrow, dear," Milena said decisively, seeing that it was already late. Vivid images had already begun to form in Milena's mind, but she managed to shoo them away until the next day.

Twelve

Irma had always thought of herself as a person who could put up with any situation, yet the sight of the squalid grey prison cell disheartened her. She had been shown in by a coarse guard who had not said a single word to her. What a life having to work in such a dreary place day in day out, she thought, almost pitying the man after he had locked the cell door. She could still feel his tight grip around her delicate arm. Of course, she had not been expecting a cordial welcome, but the whole suddenness of the situation overwhelmed her. She wept, realising this was the price she had to pay for her loose tongue. Life wasn't fair. First there was the war and then a country full of pseudo-Marxist fanatics who violated human rights. Yet she quickly realised that wallowing in self-pity wasn't going to change anything.

"So what are you in here for, comrade?" asked a woman who had just come out of the toilet.

"Telling the truth," Irma replied. She wiped her tears away, cautiously eyeing her new cellmate.

"Oh you mustn't do that with these gangsters. What kind of truth did you tell them?"

"What's it to you?"

"Well, since we're going to be spending quite some time together, I suggest you change your attitude, comrade. It'll make our lives a hell of a lot easier. But if you prefer to be nasty, then so be it," the woman said before returning to her bunk. She picked up a book and opened it at a dog-eared page.

"I'm sorry, I just can't believe all this is happening," Irma explained.

"I don't think anyone in here does, comrade," said the woman, who then turned another page. "Just don't expect things to get better too quickly."

"My name's Irma, and I'm here for having insulted the newly-appointed mayor of our village who came to confiscate most of our property in the name of communism," she confessed.

"Well, whatever you told the scoundrel, he definitely deserved it. Now, if everyone said what they really thought..." the woman began, closing her book with her forefinger as a temporary bookmark.

"Then there would be more dignity in this country, just like there had been before the war."

"No, silly, the prisons would be overcrowded. They're already full up in Prague, which is why I ended up in this hole. And you can forget about your fairy-tales from the past. The West has long given up on us."

"After they had fed us to the lions. I'm sure both Masaryks are turning in their graves."

"You won't see many of their like over the next few generations. I'm Blanka, by the way."

"Pleased to meet you. And what was your 'crime', if I may ask?" asked Irma boldly. "Were you also a victim of the party's rigid nationalisation scheme?"

"No, it was much worse than that!"

"You didn't kill a high-ranking communist party official, did you?"

"No, but I was the mistress of one," she revealed.

"Surely that's not a crime! Especially if you two only..."

she stopped, not knowing exactly how to express what she wanted to say.

"No, but selling information to a British spy is," she said offhandedly.

"They exist?"

"They're ten a penny according to my old lover. Some of them are actually cooperating with our lot, believe it or not."

"How did you happen to meet one?" Irma was curious to know.

"You don't just happen to meet a spy anywhere, for he usually finds you. If he needs to, that is," she said dryly.

"So they work together?"

"Most of them just swap information for what it's worth. The British usually want lists of official party members, so they know precisely which defectors to reject. They are basically on the lookout for anyone who's likely to worm their way into significant areas of the government. Occasionally one of them even starts secretly cooperating with the enemy. It's a dirty business," she concluded, shaking her head.

"So how and why did you get involved?"

"There's money to be made."

"I see."

"And money that's worth more than our doomed crown. If the Party really goes ahead with its preposterous currency reform next year, then it soon won't be worth the paper it's printed on."

"Currency reform?"

"The worst of its kind. But you really don't want to know what's awaiting us economically. And that wasn't the only reason, my naïve friend. There's always an outside chance of being able to flee to the West if you play your cards right. On top of all that, my spy was rather handsome."

"So what went wrong? How did you end up behind bars?"

"Well, it turned out that the one I chose just wanted some crumpet on the side. You see, he was already married, and of course, when I found out, I was so furious that I denounced him to my former Czech lover."

"I'm sure he can't have been too thrilled about that. My God, what happened then?"

"Well, there were some interrogations alright, yet I'm the only one still suffering the consequences. That'll teach me for being so impetuous. As for Mr Douglas Watkins, my two-faced spy, he was released after they made some kind of political deal."

"And you ended up in here!"

"Fraternising with the enemy, double-dealing, counter-revolutionary intentions, high treason; it's a wonder they didn't send me straight to Siberia! And to think I was so close to freedom. Lord knows what will become of me if I ever get out of here. Well, that's what you get for trying to make too much hay when the sun shines."

"How long are you in here for?"

"I was sentenced to an unspecified number of years in prison, which means they'll probably let me rot in here until I have to make room for more decadent intellectual dissidents such as yourself."

"Thanks for the compliment."

"Just be glad I've stopped calling you comrade, Irma; it means I trust you."

"Shouldn't we be careful what we say to each other? They're probably listening to our conversation right now!"

"They wouldn't waste their time on people who are already locked up. My old lover told me that."

"What kind of things did you tell this Mr Watkins?"

"You're a curious one, aren't you? Well, I suppose there's no danger now," said Blanka almost indifferently. "After falling for this gentleman, I openly told him about unofficial goings-on in the Party hierarchy and their abuse of state funds. And you'd be surprised how unfaithful most of them are. Douglas was extremely skilled at making me divulge sensitive information during unguarded moments; well he was a trained spy after all. Anyway, I'm sure he must have known that I was in a relationship with a communist official, as he tried to extract as much information out of me as possible."

"And being in love, you complied, I imagine."

"Well, I still had some delicate information up my sleeve. But I wasn't going to reveal anything else until I was a hundred percent sure of his feelings for me."

"And he said he'd do anything for you?"

"He even started telling me about his home town and how I'd like it there, but love is blind and no guarantee of getting me out of this forsaken country. Anyway, I eventually let on about the Czechs having managed to plant a mole in the British Cabinet."

"You're joking! Now this really is intriguing. How did you get hold of such information anyway? Was your ex-lover so careless?"

"He was when his hormones were out of control. On one occasion he was in such high spirits after a meeting he had attended that I was determined to find out why. You never know, I thought at the time, it may turn out to be useful. A lot of good it did me in the end! Anyway, despite getting him drunk during dinner, he was still unwilling to say anything. Drastic measures were called for, so after an evening of mutual pleasure, I succeeded in wheedling the information out of him. Men can be quite stupid at times," she said shaking her head. "All he managed to say in his blissful stupor was 'Mum's the word!' before he fell asleep."

"Didn't he regret it afterwards?"

"I don't think so. He could hardly recall the events the following day. And he probably would have lost his job if he *had* remembered and started telling everyone how foolish he had been."

"And did your Douglas chap reward you for such juicy information?"

"Well, he first turned rather pale, then clearly started to panic, which was so unlike his usual phlegmatic British demeanour. Then he asked me if I knew the name of the mole, yet I told him that I honestly didn't."

"Didn't you realise how serious the matter was?"

"I was only concerned about myself, Irma, just like the other rotten half of our population. In fact, I'm sure some of them would condemn their colleagues or denounce their own relatives if need be!"

"I don't understand the world either," Irma said in a lugubrious way after a pause. "But, come to think of it, your English friend had no other choice but to report it back home."

"And that's precisely what he tried to do, yet I was only thinking of myself and not questions of national security. In any case, he made some excuse about not wanting to be late for a class."

"He was a teacher as well?"

"Posing as one to allay the authorities' suspicions."

"But he didn't really go to work, did he?"

"I thought nothing of it, but it eventually occurred to me that he normally didn't teach on that particular day, so I went straight to his flat and caught him in the door just in time. He had packed his bags and was clearly taken aback to see me."

"He must have been. What did he say when he saw you?"

"He told me about his wife and how she'd been taken ill just before she was about to give birth, and that he had to go to her. While I stood there speechless, he finally told me that it was over between us," Blanka said sadly.

"Do you think he was telling the truth?"

"Whether he had fabricated the story or not, I'll never know, but he handed me a wad of banknotes and ran down the stairs."

"I felt so betrayed I threw the money after him and threatened to wreak vengeance on him. He simply ignored me and hastily made his way out of the building, leaving me there in tears."

"Oh dear," said Irma empathetically.

"If only I had known better," Blanka said bitterly, and then shook her head. "I could have found another spy or God knows what else!"

"Your emotions simply got the better of you. How did you meet this Mr Watkins anyway?"

"Being a spy, it had probably come to his attention that I was still regularly seeing Tlačenka. Oh, that's the name of my ex-lover, by the way. So it was imperative for him that we met. I had often attended courses organised by the British Council, and knew that their teachers often spent their time at the Kavárna Paddington on Opatovická Street, so I occasionally went there with a girlfriend of mine for a beer after class. So you see, I couldn't have made it any easier for him to make my acquaintance."

"Who made the first move?"

"He came up to me one evening, asking if my friend and I would join him and another teacher in a game of Scrabble of all things," she explained.

"What's that?"

"I didn't know either at the time, but they had borrowed it from an American colleague who was promoting this new board game all about making words out of random letters. In any case it wasn't long before we got the general hang of it."

"When did you find out he was a spy?"

"He was a brilliant actor, and it actually took a few months before he entrusted me with the information, yet by this time we had already been sleeping with one another."

"Talking about sleep, Blanka, I'm dead tired. I'd love to hear more, but let's continue tomorrow," Irma suggested.

Listening to Blanka's misfortunes was like walking straight into a spider's web. Instead of becoming mortified and doing everything to disentangle herself from the sticky fibres, Irma was willingly becoming a part of the web, watching as the spider moved from one end to another, vying for her constant attention. This wasn't difficult as Irma was both patient and curious. Over the next few weeks, Irma realised that she herself was quite good at extracting information out of her cellmate. For all its dubiousness, it made the time pass more quickly, and Blanka obviously found it therapeutic to regurgitate the whole experience, which made Irma feel like some kind of therapist. Irma found the whole affair so compelling, so unlike anything in her wildest dreams, in fact, that she became intent on writing about it once her sentence was over. Of course, it was impossible to take notes in prison, so she would have to rely on her memory, which wouldn't be a problem. If there were one thing she was good at, it was learning things by heart.

Thirteen

"Wow, what a story!" Lucinda exclaimed as she hung onto Milena's every word.

"Poor Blanka, however, had no desire to be caught up in the world of espionage," said Milena solemnly, "but the last we heard, something dreadful had happened to her in prison."

"Not quite the happy ending you'd expect, is it?"

"Well, she was playing with fire, but it doesn't all end there, my dear. Irma's lucky not to have succumbed to a similar fate herself, as the English spies knew that she had struck up a friendship with Blanka in jail, which meant that she was suddenly a potential security risk," Milena explained.

"And all because this Douglas chap had abandoned Blanka," Lucinda surmised.

"Well, in a way I can understand his actions, as he didn't really have any other choice, did he?"

It would be all too easy to label Douglas as a conniving agent, Lucinda realised. Of course, he did everything possible to find out as much as he could from Blanka, for his superiors had after all instructed him to do so. And he was well aware of the fact that their days were numbered, but everything was going so splendidly. Blanka's knowledge was indispensable to his country's security. Douglas was the first of his colleagues to learn what really went on behind closed doors as well as which English spies were secretly working for the Czechs, so he naively hoped things would simply continue the way they were, especially seeing that he had started to become emotionally involved with Blanka. Yet, one day it all came to an abrupt end when she informed him of the biggest secret the Czechs possessed. It was their one unparalleled advantage over the British government. A secret for which Blanka, however, would end up paying dearly. This must have made her ponder all the other wrong turns she had taken in her life.

Lucinda's eyes widened.

"A mole in the British Cabinet?"

"Exactly, and a highly-placed one at that!"

"So who was it?"

"Blanka had no inkling of who it was; only the fact that he was there. He was probably some kind of minister or something. I guess we'll never know."

"And that's why they killed Blanka?" Lucinda asked in bewilderment.

"Well, it was never really clear who was responsible for her death. For their part, the British had been desperate to prevent this information from leaking at all costs, regardless of who it actually was. You see, the fact that a mole had reached such a high position was an outright embarrassment not only for the whole country but for the individuals responsible as well. If any of this had been made public at the time, the government along with its secret service would have been discredited, people would have lost their jobs and their pensions; heads would have rolled! So even if they eventually found out who the mole was, the whole affair had to be hushed up for decades to come; it probably still is, unless Irma's spy friend has broken his silence in the meantime," explained Milena.

"Don't tell me she also started playing scrabble with fake English teachers!"

"No, I don't think that was the tried and tested pattern, but it wasn't long before they dragged her into it. Yet, she hardly expected things to turn out the way they did, especially so soon after being released from prison."

"How terrible! But hang on, that must have been how she got to England in the first place," deduced Lucinda.

"Yes, but it could have all backfired, my dear. We can just thank God that she got out of it alive."

"They probably thought she knew who the mole was, the poor dear!"

"Hm, that's what Irma told me at first, but that information is irrelevant when it's a matter of safeguarding a state secret."

"So what happened when she came home from prison?"

"She spent most of her time writing as if there were no tomorrow. She said she had to note everything down before time eventually erased it from her memory. It's a wonder that she could remember as much as she did."

"Did she leave any of her diaries behind?"

"She took most of what she had with her, so you'll most likely find everything with her in England, but she did leave one diary behind. I'll show it to you once I find it again," Milena promised.

"What did she do apart from writing? Did she find a job?"

"She was an enemy of the state, a so-called potential counter-revolutionary imperialist, so they would never entrust her with a normal job. She had no other option but to help out with the running of the collective farm, which included both manual work in the fields as well as a bit of accounting, which was just recording how much food was produced every month, making sure the figures matched up with those stipulated in the government's five-year agricultural plan," Milena said, shaking her head.

"And did the figures ever add up?"

"In ninety percent of farms they didn't, and the other ten percent were presumably manipulating their figures."

"Well, at least you had a part of your own farm, so to speak," Lucinda said, trying to look on the bright side.

"When there was enough food it was fine, otherwise we had to rely on our grandparents in the east; somehow they always managed to have plenty of food no matter how rough the times were," Milena said.

"They must have experienced a great slab of history."

"Klara lives on their old farm in Luhačovice near the Slovakian border. You must visit her one day."

"Oh, I'd love to."

Fourteen

Sarah always loved driving out to her grandparents' place in Healesville. Well, once the suburbs were behind her, she did.

"They just can't get enough," she blurted out in indignation from the back seat.

"What's that, dear?" her mother Emma asked.

"When are they finally going to stop?"

"Stop what?"

"Just look at all those houses," she went on.

"What's wrong with them?"

"They're everywhere!" Sarah complained bitterly. "And there are more being built every time we drive up this way. Locusts!"

"We're in the suburbs, Sarah," Emma rationalised.

"You don't understand, Mum. All this used to be gorgeous bush land."

"I don't know what you're complaining about, it's lovely here," William said, interrupting her. His tolerance knew no bounds, which is what Sarah liked about her father, but she knew she could never be like him.

"Well, what's left of it. It was twice this size five years ago!"

"C'mon, the people have to live somewhere. The population of Melbourne is constantly growing," he said.

"At an unprecedented exponential rate," she added.

"And what do you propose they do?" Emma objected. "You can't keep them cramped up in the cities, Sarah."

"Just because there are empty paddocks and fields doesn't mean you can simply build on them! We're not in Hong Kong or New York, you know. And most of it used to be pure unadulterated nature, full of kangaroos, grazing sheep, birds..."

"Not forgetting all the snakes!" William added.

"Oh, I can do without them," Emma said, shuddering at the thought.

"Well, they're not actually waiting out there to pounce on you. They just go about their business, following their instincts, which probably helps keep them away from us."

"I suppose you're right, dear," concluded Emma as they embarked on the long-awaited winding, picturesque drive through open plains and eucalyptus forests. She and her parents hardly exchanged a word during the rest of the trip, so everyone was left to their own thoughts. Emma was preoccupied with her father-in-law's health. Even though at eighty-nine he was still fit, old age had nevertheless started to take its toll. His voice had changed, he had become a bit too forgetful and he no longer batted an eyelid about things that would normally have sent him flying into a rage in the past. Emma's husband William, who had quickly learned how to stop worrying ever since coming to Australia, took each day as it came. He was happy that there wasn't much traffic on the roads and that he could look forward to watching his favourite football team play against the team George keenly followed that evening on television. Even Sarah was in her own world, soaking up all the rural impressions through the window of the car. It did wonders for her creativity. If only I could have lived in the late nineteenth century, long before the advent of sprawling suburbs and rapid development, she mused. I'm sure this country's great impressionist masters would hardly be able to recognise, let alone approve of the places they had once painted, so much have they been transformed. They are probably turning in their graves. Of course, they couldn't reach these places as fast as we can today – a short train ride today could have meant a whole day's journey in their day – but I'm sure they didn't feel the need to rush about like headless chooks the way we do nowadays.

"Your father has started to write his autobiography of all things!" Emma said to her husband out of the blue as they were approaching Healesville. "He told me last night when I asked him what was new."

"Well, he has to do something now they've sold their tea rooms," William said.

"Did he do anything else besides teaching English to new immigrants?" asked Sarah.

"Not that I know of," William admitted. "He rarely talked about his work, but I doubt whether he had any other duties. George used to tell his friends that he was 'drilling English grammar into Melbourne's growing population.' Well, he knew he had a job for life. Yet I can't remember much else about it while I was growing up. All I cared about was playing football, and then all of a sudden I found myself back in England again, studying in Exeter."

"Poor gran," Sarah began, "left all alone in the country, making Devonshire tea for all those day trippers."

"Oh, don't you worry about my mother; she enjoyed chatting her time away with the guests. Many were regulars from the village, so she was hardly ever alone. Anyway, be glad I left Australia back then, otherwise I would never have met *your* mother!"

"I'm eternally grateful to destiny," she said rather flippantly.

"It's George you should thank. He always feared that I'd be sent to Vietnam in the late sixties, which definitely would have postponed my studies, and well…could even have proven to be fatal," he said in reflection. William looked fondly through the windscreen at the familiar places of days long gone.

"Wise old Bedřich!" Sarah said, and smiled as she gazed at the countless trees that lined their grandparents' street. She wondered for how much longer she would be able to enjoy this experience, seeing that her grandparents were both almost ninety. On this occasion it was her grandfather's birthday. Even though his name was George, she called him 'Bedřich' since he was very fond of the composer Smetana. She knew that he had worked as an English teacher in Czechoslovakia in the early fifties, prior to emigrating to Australia. He must have become exposed to Czech classical music while he was probably drilling the intricacies of English grammar into the Czechs, she concluded. In any case, I'm sure he has enough anecdotes to fill a whole book, which should keep him busy for the next couple of years, I imagine. Perhaps he'll even let me read it one day.

Fifteen

Mr Thaunton was trying to concentrate on the individual lines of each page of the novel he was reading. He was sitting on a crowded train on his way to university as the second half of the academic year was just about to begin. Every time he reached the end of the lines at the lower end of the right hand pages, his attention would meander to the colourful ringed stockings of the woman sitting diagonally opposite him. He tried to make out all the tones which were predominantly blue: royal blue, petrol blue, bluish-grey... She seemed way too restless for his liking, constantly crossing and uncrossing her legs, rubbing her knees despite the heating on the train. Cobalt blue, navy blue, turquoise, ultramarine, he continued musing. Just as he was running out of blue hues, he heard the besuited man opposite him loudly turn and skilfully fold the pages of his newspaper. The silence that briefly resumed as the man began studying the financial section was broken again by the shrill ringtone of his mobile phone. Pages suddenly fluttered like the wings of pigeons, and the smell of newspaper ink filled the air. Mr Thaunton's nose twitched uncomfortably as the man answered his phone.

"Hel-lo? Oh, it's you," he began. "No I'm still on the train. Hmm? No, I just decided to catch up on some sleep given that this morning's meeting had been cancelled. Anyway Sarah, we still need to go through the points of that contract…"

The name suddenly made Mr Thaunton think of his favourite student. He struggled to focus his attention on page seventy-nine of the book. It was a right-hand page, and the other commuter started to warm her hands between her knees. Petrol blue was definitely his favourite colour. The woman was also wearing a blue jumper and a jeans miniskirt under her brown suede jacket. Fashion-wise, his type of girl really, yet he was in no mood to strike up a conversation that she probably wouldn't welcome anyway. She'd be ideal in a commercial for blueberries, he thought as his attention strayed once again.

"We basically negotiate for them and they have very little say in the matter…"

The words blurred and for a while Mr Thaunton's mind filled with images of his and Sarah's brief encounters in and out of class until the man's voice became noticeably louder.

"Yes, I know they may kick up a fuss, but it's your job to get them to sign under our conditions, okay?"

Mr Thaunton sighed, and as the train coasted towards Flinders Street Station, he wondered what Sarah was going to be wearing in class that day.

Sixteen

Having spent most of the week in bed on account of a bout of flu, Sarah cursed every time she sneezed or had to blow her sore, red nose. She wasn't very good at suffering. 'A typical Aries!' her mother Emma would say as she looked after her one and only daughter. As a protective mother, she always knew what was best and insisted her daughter sleep at their family home in Eltham until she recovered properly. So Sarah found herself in her comfortable single bed that seemed to belong to another era. Nevertheless, she was fond of her old bedroom with its window facing the garden. She felt she couldn't stand any more chicken soup, even though she knew it was doing her cold a world of good. She was staring at the bare fruit trees in their garden, wondering when they would be ripe with apricots again, when thoughts of her missed classes popped into her mind, as well as someone she now wouldn't see until next week. She cursed again, went back under the sheets and slowly drifted into a deep sleep.

The Indian myna landed on the edge of the fence and pondered the garden whose existence seemed to be solely for it to behold and enjoy. It moved its head erratically from side to side in a way that only birds can, and it wasn't long before the fruit tree caught its omnivorous attention. Although the opulent tree was only about one and a half metres high, individual branches were already laden with ripe fruit ready for picking. Emma was especially looking forward to using the fruit in the apricot tart that she was famous for. She was in the habit of inviting a few close friends over for coffee and cakes every Sunday, a ritual she had grown up with and kept up over the years.

"Be a dear, Sarah, and get me some apricots from the tree before they completely foul away. You know how impossible it is to wheedle your father into doing anything these days!"

"Sure, I was going outside anyway to paint part of our garden in a Pierre Bonnard sort of way."

"Pierre who?" enquired Sarah's mother, not having the faintest idea about the painters that had inspired her daughter ever since she had taken up painting. Then it was just a hobby, now it seemed like an existential necessity to her. And to think she gave up a perfectly good teaching career to go back to university to study art instead of something serious, her mother often grumbled.

"I've got a print of his *Blooming almond tree* on the back of my door, you know the one."

"That's nice dear, about fifteen should do, love."

"Fifteen?"

"Apricots, dear! Best get them before you start painting, as I've got the dough almost finished."

"Okay, I'll just get my easel and colours first." Sarah sighed as she made her way to her bedroom.

William Hafner was always in the habit of leaving everything till the last minute, thus allowing the odd bird to be dazzled by the sight of so many resplendent apricots. So instead of gathering all the tempting fruit in time, most of it ended up being randomly pecked at by the discerning bird kingdom of their neighbourhood.

Descending onto the grass, the conniving intruder hopped towards what it must have regarded as its next meal, yet as it approached, ready to lunge at a piece of succulent fruit, its yellow beak just bounced back. It tried its luck several more times on different parts of the tree, but to no avail. The confused bird then leaped into flight, frantically flapping its wings for a few moments above the tree to scrutinize the situation. Settling on one of the wooden posts that lay across the top of the tree, it stuck out its mask-like head that protruded from its brown body, renewing a flurry of attempts to get at the object of its desires. Yet the strong net that William had resolutely placed around the wooden posts continued to frustrate the bird's endeavours, causing it to twitter lividly. So alluring was the fragrance of the fruit that the bird began to pull at the threads of the net with its sharp beak. Eventually a gap had opened small enough to enable the hungry bandit to slip its head through and start gorging on bits of the fruit. It hung there in a droll manner for a while before manoeuvring its way through the net completely.

Carrying her easel and colours, Sarah opened the back door that closed behind her with a loud whoosh. Still oblivious to the winged culprit's initial triumph, she started to adjust the height of her easel. Meanwhile the feathered fiend was not only enjoying mini chunks of a random apricot, it was also causing others to fall to the ground. Up above, nebulous clouds scudded across a carefree sky. A gentle breeze scattered Sarah's thoughts and she forgot for a while where she was, thereby allowing another dream to force its arbitrary way into her mind. Bygone days in Devon suddenly appeared, rekindling misty memories of lazy summers spent with her best friend Lucinda as they were growing up together. She temporarily revelled in the vivid images of them mischievously playing and marvelling at the world around them in nearby Shaldon, interwoven with eye-opening moments of another kind...

"Lucinda, stop playing with your food! You've got sauce all over your cheeks. Sarah, behave or I'll tell your mother!" warned Mrs Vánočka in a reprimanding way.

"We were only playing," said Lucinda innocently.

"Throwing food about like that is not playing, young lady," continued Lucinda's mother. "Now eat the rest of your lunch or there won't be any dessert for either of you today," she said on her way out of the kitchen.

"Do you remember the time we poked our fingers in all those cream cakes? There must have been over ten of them."

"Poor mum, I can't remember her having been more cross with us; she hasn't been back to that cake shop ever since."

"We were only five and all we wanted to do was to taste them," began Lucinda, "I can still remember licking all that cream and icing off my fingers to get rid of the evidence..."

Then you place your third finger here, and your little finger there. What a strange chord shape, thought Sarah to herself as she tried to strum the chord without making the strings buzz too much. Really, it's enough to make your fingers ache. All these sequences of chords: *Gmaj7, Am7b5, D7b9, B flat diminished* or was it *half-diminished*? Bother! Why did he absolutely have to teach me such difficult chords today, Sarah lamented. I'm sure it was just so that he could touch my hand all the more. Why didn't I learn all this when I was younger, with lots of time to kill? Could have been really good by now. All those wasted years sleeping till midday; watching moronic TV shows, or hanging out with all those deranged friends after school. Now, my children will have none of that! Their time will be put to better use, she declared. I'll make them learn at least four languages, a classical instrument; if it's a girl, she'll do ballet, and if it's a…no, on second thoughts, not at all keen on a boy. Too boisterous for my sensitive nerves…although, you can't really give it back if it turns out to be one, can you? Nevertheless, I recently heard somewhere that having sex shortly after ovulating results in a girl most of the time. Hmm, what was that nice-sounding chord again? *E7b5*, which apparently is the same as *E7#11* for some reason. At least he could have made a pass at me when he had his hand around my hips! What was he waiting for? A green light? Or some kind of fanfare, for heaven's sake! Pity, there's now no one else to share this newly-discovered sound with. Maybe I could make grumpy bear smile (chord resonates, but no response). Not even a twitch! C'mon, bear, give me a smile, please! Hmm, perhaps I'll get a reaction from my plants; maybe they'll even grow better. I wonder what would happen if I played badly, though. It might possibly scare away all those horrid tiny insects that appear every now and then. Yet must be careful not to sound discordant; wouldn't want to traumatise the poor dears, would we now. I'm sure the camellia in particular can feel the vibration of every string being plucked. I'm sure he finds me attractive, Sarah mused as her right hand delved between her legs. She gently began caressing herself. She allowed the guitar to fall and pressed herself closer to the back of the guitar's smooth neck until her whole body quivered with delight.

"Dinner's ready!" announced Emma loudly from the kitchen. Sarah awoke feeling extremely uncomfortable; her body was covered in sweat. She peeled off her soaked pyjamas, and as she made her way to the bathroom, fleeting images of herself playing the guitar to her old teddy bear and of a bird devouring apricots filled her mind. She felt relieved under the shower, it was almost like being reborn.

"Feeling better?" asked Emma as she served dinner.

"Much better, I think I'll go to work tomorrow," she said before coughing several times and clearing her throat.

"You'll do no such thing until you're a hundred percent fit!" her mother decided.

"Oh, I'll be okay."

"We'll see about that."

"By the way, did you know that your new cactus and lavender-smelling soap contains a substance called Methyl-chloroisothiazolinone?" asked Sarah, slowly reading the name of the strange ingredient printed on the package.

"What on earth is that?"

"Haven't the faintest, yet it doesn't sound too healthy, does it?" she said, coughing once more.

"Neither do you, dear."

Seventeen

Grglrlgrl grlg! Grrgrglrlrglrl! Lucinda's throat ached. She could scarcely talk after having pushed her vocal chords to the limits that evening at one of her band's weekly rehearsals. She'd inadvertently overstrained her voice while trying to sing one of their jazz songs in the original key, because Pavel the guitarist had been too lazy to transpose the chords. They had churned out one song too many that evening, and now Lucinda found herself adding an overflowing teaspoonful of honey to her mallow tea. Some of the lyrics still resounded in her head: *Every time we meet my heart skips a few beats now, oh yeah!* She cupped her chin in her left hand while her free hand listlessly stirred the tea. *I wanna be beside you, never leave or do without your love.* Her little finger scraped up the spilled honey on the table. She watched it run down the inside of her hand before licking up the sticky substance. Bloody nails! Why do they have to grow so fast, she asked herself. *Kiss and make love to me, for I'm a wild pulsating heart.* After she had taken several sips of the soothing potion, she asked herself whether it was really worth all the bother. Not that she was considering giving up her newly-found hobby of singing altogether, she just felt besieged with doubts. At each rehearsal, however, she regained her desire to sing and was redeemed with a surge of exhilaration as she did her best to learn all the songs in the band's repertoire. All hyped up, she would then go home to paint as a way of exhausting her energy. If sleep eluded her once she was in bed, she often caressed herself in order to release any pent-up tensions that were still channelling their way through her system.

Lucinda's life had become increasingly solitary, since she had felt little sense in becoming romantically involved with someone just for the sake of being in a relationship. Her friends, on the other hand, seemed unable to discuss anything else, dwelling mostly on the harrowing aspects of togetherness. Still, she listened to both her friends' lamentations as well as their joys, which more often than not revolved around sexual pleasure. In any case, Lucinda was intent on not letting romance encumber her independence or diminish her inspiration to paint. One day she would return to England anyway and what then? Apart from that, emotions usually wreaked havoc on her creativity. Life as a single also meant that she had more time on her hands and she soon noticed that painting alone could not entirely use up her abundant supply of energy. She resolved to do something about it. The telephone suddenly rang, extinguishing all her thoughts.

"Oh dear, you sound worse than I do... No problem, we can swap shifts. What time? As early as that? Okay, don't worry, I'll manage somehow... Now you take care and get well soon!"

Realising now that she had to get up earlier than expected, Lucinda set her alarm clock, gulped down the rest of her tea, and eventually fell into a blissful sleep.

Eighteen

"Wakey-wakey!" said a cheerful voice behind the door.

"Ugh," moaned Sarah grumpily, "just a few more minutes, please!" pleaded Sarah, not quite convinced that she'd had enough sleep.

"Well it is already after eleven o'clock, for your information," announced Emma after slowly opening her daughter's bedroom door. "You can't stay in bed all day, or you'll be up all night!"

Her mother's voice was far too kind to disagree with, so she got up and kissed her smiling cheeks.

"Good morning, mother. I don't know what I'd do without you," she said yawning and stretching her arms.

"You'd still be asleep no doubt," she said, before opening the curtains abruptly. The room was suddenly flooded with bright light, which made Sarah squint.

"Yeah, I guess it is a bit late for beauty sleep, isn't it?" she reasoned.

"Don't know what you're worried about; even first thing out of bed you're as pretty as a picture."

"Well the long sleep seems to have finally cured me of this wretched cold."

"And you look much better too, so greet this brand new day with all its challenges, demands and opportunities!"

"Hello day!" she cried out, crossing her arms as she half-heartedly looked out of the window. "I think I'll go for a jog before I have breakfast," she said while she started to get changed into her grey tracksuit pants and her rose-coloured fleecy hoodie, zipping it right up to her neck.

"Lunch, you mean! It'll be ready soon, so don't eat too much."

"I'll just have a cup of tea, then," she said, still yawning.

"Okay, you go for a run, and I'll have the tea ready for you when you get back."

"Thanks, mum!"

Being the epitome of a selfless parent, Emma's words of wisdom or consolation accompanied Sarah as the years went on. She appreciated all her mother's little insights about life's intricate moments and phases every time she confided her wishes, ambitions and fears to her. When she started to take an interest in the opposite sex, Sarah would talk freely about matters of the heart, but somehow she hesitated to say anything about her infatuation with her favourite teacher. Perhaps she was afraid that her mother might somehow talk her out of it or make her feel that she was behaving in a frivolous manner.

Jogging in the fields behind the house was doing her a world of good. It eventually made her decide to write to Mr Thaunton. Perhaps a chain of email exchanges could bring us closer together or even spark off something special, she mused optimistically. The fresh air spurred her into action. She ran inside the house and made her way to the kitchen, where, as promised, a pot of tea was awaiting her. She poured herself a cup and hurried back into her room, hastily switching on the computer. As her outdated operating system was noisily starting up, she sipped at her tea. It warmed her stomach and briefly stopped the pangs of hunger she usually felt in the morning. She gave her computer a swift kick and it gradually stopped howling, and silently hummed away in the background.

After logging into her account, she hesitated, for she didn't really know what she wanted to say. Coming up with good ideas wasn't easy on an empty stomach. Just write whatever first comes to mind, she told herself.

> From: sarahhafner@arts-stud.melbuni.com.au
> Sent: Thursday, 20.08.2015, 12:25
> To: Mr Thaunton
> Re: my absence
>
> Dear Mr Thaunton,
>
> I'm sure you're wondering why I didn't attend class last week…

No, that's too presumptuous, she pondered, and thought about writing: 'In case you were wondering' instead, but it somehow didn't sound right either. She tried once again.

> Due to a nasty cold I had all week, I wasn't able to attend your class on Tuesday, so could you please inform me if there was any work to prepare for our next lesson? Regarding the homework we had over the break, I've written about my favourite Van Gogh paintings.

No, that sounds way too impersonal. And that would probably confuse the poor man. Hmm, she sighed and took another sip of her tea. I must try to be more natural.

> Unfortunately, I caught some awful flu last week that had me bedridden for several days at my parents' place. Seeing that I wasn't in class to present my homework,

I'm sending you this brief resume of it.

When I think of all the paintings that have influenced me in a positive way, it would be impossible for me to narrow it down to just one choice. When I was a teenager my friend's grandmother, who had also taught me how to paint by the way, took me to an exhibition of Van Gogh paintings. Even though there were hundreds of paintings on display, I think I spent an hour simply staring at four or five that I really admired for various aesthetic reasons, especially the way the paint had been applied. Not only did I become a big fan of this master's work, it was also a time when I started to take my own painting very seriously. I think it was appreciating the combination of colours the artist used, particularly in works such as *View of Arles with Irises* that proved to be pivotal in the way I depict a motive. *Daubigny's garden* and *Thatched cottages by a hill* are so lovely to gaze at, I would just love to spend a week holidaying there with someone special to forget about life for a while, revelling in the whole novelty of the situation.

Please let me know if there's anything I should prepare or read for next week. I really enjoy your lessons and would hate to fall behind. I'm feeling much better today and have been up and about, so I'm looking forward to our next class. Hope you're well.

Yours,
Sarah Hafner

Now that sounds better, she thought to herself. A bit daring though. Perhaps he'll suggest…oh stop dreaming Sarah. I'll cross that bridge if I ever get to it! Okay, so I'm completely infatuated with him. There's nothing wrong with that!

I should just enjoy this consuming feeling while I can, for everything may change once I get to know him properly. Sarah wondered how Mr Thaunton was going to interpret her piece of writing. She didn't think she was being too obvious, even though she sometimes did have an oblique way of expressing things.

Sarah's mother suddenly appeared at her door.

"Lunch is ready!" she said. "You must be starving."

"Oh it's alright, I've been distracting my stomach with my studies."

"Well, come and distract your mind for a while with some delicious schnitzels!" she insisted.

Nineteen

"You ought to be in bed, Lucinda," Sarah reprimanded her, as she coughed once again.

"I ate some daisies, so I'll soon be okay," she said, and continued to mix blue, green and a touch of maroon paint together.

"Oh gosh, you're supposed to make a tea out of the flowers, not eat them, silly!" She shook her head and started to daub the outstretched canvas with splashes of paint.

"It was you who told me it's what you take when you're ill, and so I did," she told her almost reproachfully. She dipped her brush in the turquoise-olive colour combination, and applied it to Sarah's left cheek.

"Hey, what are you doing?" Sarah was so nonplussed it took her quite a while to react. Lucinda, however, didn't hesitate to paint her other cheek, laughing aloud. "I'll show you!" Sarah finally protested, and started to chase her around the garden with her paintbrush. Lucinda fell over and Sarah got on top of her, and slowly polka-dotted her face with vermilion-coloured dabs.

"Oh my! Now you really look ill," Sarah giggled, and the two began to wrestle on the grass for a while. After a few minutes they lay on their backs exhausted, and contemplated the sky.

"We should finish painting Veronika's present, you know,"

Lucinda remarked, and when she turned on her side, she noticed that they were lying amongst hundreds of daisies. She started to rip several out of the ground with her hands and cram them into her mouth.

"Hey what are you doing? Stop it," warned Sarah. "You look pale."

"I think I'm going to be sick," she complained, and ran to fetch herself a large glass of water.

Lucinda awoke, not really feeling much better than the night before. In dire need of a pee, she ran to the bathroom.

Twenty

What a meal! Sarah thought as she helped herself to another slice of her mother's carrot cake. It was the only dessert she loved to overindulge in, thinking the carrots made it healthy in some way and neutralized the effect of the icing she covered it with. While she savoured another forkful, she couldn't stop wondering whether Mr Thaunton had had time to reply yet. Before rushing off to her room to find out, she helped her mother with the dishes. Emma wouldn't relax until everything in the kitchen was spick and span again.

"I think I'm fit enough to go back to work tomorrow," Sarah said, knowing that her mother wouldn't protest this time.

"And what are you going to do with the rest of the afternoon?" Emma asked.

"I'll probably put some finishing touches to that oasis garden painting I'm working on."

"Surely you can't mean our garden, dear?" her mother asked in astonishment.

"No, I based that painting on sketches I made in Dorothy's garden in Warrandyte. Her father really has green fingers. And they even have a fig tree!"

"Well, he can come over here anytime if he runs out of garden!"

"I'll let him know, but somehow I doubt whether…"

"And whatever became of your painting of our apricot tree from last summer?"

"I've decided to include a bird in the scene."

"Not that horrible little beast that keeps gnawing at our precious fruit?"

"No, I was thinking more of a magpie to make it clearly Australian."

"Well we do get quite a few that sing in our backyard every morning, but in the end I guess it's entirely up to you how you wish to depict reality."

Sarah liked her mother's last sentence; if only there were some way, she thought, of being able to have that same artistic freedom over one's own destiny.

"Was there anybody else in our family who painted, mum?" Sarah asked, suddenly becoming eager to know more about her family's past.

"Not that I know of," Emma began. "I think it was Irma's influence that got you started. She often looked after Lucinda and yourself when you were small. With your father and me both working and your grandparents having settled in Australia, we were glad she could take you under her wing from time to time. Anyhow, I wonder how she's doing."

"She must be over eighty by now," realised Sarah. "In any case I liked her a lot."

"And you rarely ever heard anything negative come from her lips," Emma recalled.

"Lucinda and I could really relate to her, but we found it odd that she would never say anything about her life in Czechoslovakia and how she got to England in the first place."

"Yes, it was all a bit shrouded in mystery, but I'm sure she had her reasons."

"And probably lots of dreams and ambitions that she

never told anyone about," stated Sarah as she straightened out the dish towel that had become damp from the drying.

"Don't bother hanging them up, dear; they're in need of a wash."

"So am I in fact!" Sarah said, and rushed off to the bathroom to have a hot shower.

Twenty-one

"Yeow! Fuck!" screamed Lucinda, as the water scalded her feet. She still had problems trying to work out how to regulate the water temperature from the erratic boiler. It was quite an old model, and in desperate need of maintenance. Whilst trying to find a nice medium between arctic cold and unbearably hot, she somehow managed to rinse her soapy body. And as if that wasn't enough, she almost fell over whilst trying to get out of the bathtub.

High time I moved into my own place, she thought. Can't wait to see that flat Kamila told me about.

After dressing as fast as she could, she ate a banana and gulped down her tea. Although she had overslept, a quick glance at the clock reassured her that she could still make it to work on time, provided that the number 6 tram was just as tardy as she was. She brushed her teeth so quickly, it made her wonder whether it had any effect apart from freshening her breath. As she frantically rushed out of the door, she recognised her name on a thick padded envelope that was sticking out of Kamila's letterbox. After managing to carefully pull it out intact, she made her way down to the tram stop. She sighed in relief as she saw a belated tram slowly coming around the corner. Once on the tram she opened the envelope to discover a faded old notebook and a letter from Milena.

Podbřežice, 19th August, 2015

Dear Lucinda,

It was so nice getting to know you better. Seeing that you showed quite an interest in your grandmother Irma, I had a proper look around her old room and in the library, and found a diary from 1953. Perhaps it can fill the gaps in the story that I wasn't able to.

Klara is looking forward to meeting you, too, so let her know when you'd like to visit her. And feel free to visit me any time again. I'll make you those fruit dumplings I promised you last time!

Take care.
Milena

How nice of her, thought Lucinda as the tram rumbled through the streets, clanging its bell every time it neared a stop to warn pedestrians who either weren't looking where they were going or had their eyes glued to their phones. Lucinda arrived at her stop and walked the rest of the way to the café. When she came to its entrance, she stopped to look inside through the large window. The café was empty. Hope I didn't rush for nothing, she thought, and frowned, pressing her lips tightly together in a grimace. She tried the door handle and it opened. Oh good, at least the owner must be around. Before she entered, she took a few steps back and observed herself briefly in the café's huge front window, wondering whether she looked presentable after such a harrowing night.

Twenty-two

The wind howled and the raindrops lashed against the café's two front windows, blurring the inside of the café and making it look like an impressionist painting to passers-by.

As she gathered empty cups and glasses, Sarah couldn't help but catch brief snatches of the conversations around her.

"I smeared a bit of the cream around the infected area inside contrary to my gynaecologist's instructions and the warning inside the packet, yet it really helped! And all those funny rashes soon disappeared."

"Imagine, it's minus fourteen degrees, you're hopelessly lost, trying to work out which *Strasse* you are on in order to find the bloody place, and just as you begin typing a text message, the screen of your phone just cracks!"

"Three more lattes, please," ordered a long-haired student who had been immersed in a discussion on an obscure literary theme with two other students he was sitting with. Sarah couldn't help but listen in on their conversation, which she quickly shrugged off as academic gobbledegook.

"You see, he deliberately deceives the reader with his cultivated elusiveness and discursive narrative. It forms the very basis of his later works, of course," one of them continued confidently.

"Of course!" whispered Sarah to herself as she wandered

to another table, gathering more empty cups and plates full of countless crumbs, the remnants of this morning's freshly-baked cheesecake that her boss proudly boasted was the best this side of Carlton and beyond.

"It cured me in three days and we've been having wild sex ever since! The other day, for instance…"

I really don't want to know, thought Sarah to herself. Please don't go into any details!

"It still made the beep sounds as I pressed the buttons, but you can't really do much without the screen, can you?"

"All the variegated elements of her ultimate transgression unexpectedly coalesce into abhorrent abjection. The whole spectre of prescient literature is quite a ubiquitous phenomenon actually," added the student who had just ordered more coffee.

Oh, do impart some of the wealth of your accumulated knowledge unto us unworthy humble beings, thought Sarah incredulously, before turning her attention to another couple that had strayed into the café in a successful attempt to escape the inclement weather. It had started to pour in the meantime, making Elgin Street glisten with raindrops. Sarah gave them a welcoming smile.

How can you consume so much caffeine, thought Sarah, shaking her head as she prepared to make another round for the loquacious latte addicts. Their blood pressure must be through the roof, she figured. Being very observant, Sarah loved to watch all the little rituals the café-dwellers would go through before actually drinking their coffees. She felt they said a lot about a particular person's character. The people who had time on their hands would either move their spoons around the rims of their cups in half-circles, or skim the surface of their beverage with the underside of their spoons, some careful not to spoil the fancy frothy arrangements. While they relished their treats, gently scooping out parts of the froth that were sprinkled with chocolate, there were others who would simply plunge their spoons into their coffees and give them a rigorous stir before unceremoniously gulping down their muddy brews.

Even though Sarah liked her job, she wondered how long this *brief* stint as a waitress was going to last. Surely not for the entire duration of my studies, she thought, suddenly becoming dismayed. And as if trying to shoo away this inauspicious prospect, she looked on the bright side of her job. For all its stultifying aspects, it not only kept her financially afloat, it also gave her the opportunity to adorn the café's walls with her works. She only ever managed to sell the odd painting or two, as she was reluctant to part with her oeuvres unless the price was appropriate. Purchases were thus rare, as the 'appropriate' price was normally out of her guests' budget range. Nevertheless, there were exceptions as one customer unexpectedly proved to her on that very day.

"I just love your use of colours, they seem to dance before my eyes, evoking images of something that seems to be missing in my life." The way the man looked at her as he praised her work made her wonder whether he was more interested in her than what she had painted, so she passed him a flyer which included a brief description of each painting on sale and its price. She noticed his eyes widen a fraction.

"Fair enough," he said in a nonchalant way, which in turn made Sarah's eyes widen noticeably. "I'll come back when I've got more money on me. Would you mind reserving it for me till the end of the exhibition?"

"Sure," she said brightly, "will happily do so." So apparently you do meet people with money to throw around, thought Sarah.

"It must be marvellous to be able to produce such art, but how do you know when a particular painting is finished?" he asked curiously.

"It's probably something inside me that luckily knows when it's time to stop. I guess it's some kind of primal intuition."

"Excuse me, are those lattes going to take long?" one of the students asked impatiently from a neighbouring table, which came as unannounced as an alarm clock, and Sarah suddenly realised her actual role in the café again.

"Coming!" she said rather briskly before turning to her art lover. "Is there anything else I can get *you*?"

"Just the bill, thanks."

After bringing the academic trio their coffees, which they eagerly started sipping to fuel more babble, she quickly took the newcomers' order. The art lover paid, and Sarah made her way to the kitchen. Time to check my emails while nobody's around, she thought mischievously as she logged into her account and impatiently scanned the flickering screen. Noticing that there was indeed a new message from her teacher, she clicked on it, and her eyes devoured every single word.

From: thaunton@arts-fac.melbuni.com.au
Sent: Saturday, 22.08.2015, 11:25
To: Sarah Hafner
Re: Last lesson

Dear Sarah,

I'm also a big Van Gogh fan. If only such places still existed the way he painted them!

Although it was pleasing in our last lesson to hear all the contributions from the students, it was astounding to see just how different tastes in art can be. I especially enjoyed seeing Dorothy's aunt's painting from the sixties.

Otherwise, you didn't really miss out on any course work. I didn't set any homework but urged the students to go and see the impressionist collections on display on the second floor of the National Gallery in town and report on one painting that particularly appealed to them. So if you can manage to visit the gallery before our next lesson on Tuesday, I'd love to hear your thoughts. Also good to hear you're well again.

Kind regards,
Thaunton

Squealing with delight, Sarah covered her mouth, as there were still quite a few guests in the café. She felt it had become eerily silent, so she took a peek in their direction. Nothing out of the ordinary. She shuffled through the café's vast CD collection. Her smile broadened when she chanced upon Elgar's Cello Concerto, and she hastily placed it into the CD player. Feeling exhilarated as the first strokes of the cello resounded within the café's walls, she fondly reminisced how she once got close to having an orgasm whilst on a date at a concert featuring Elgar's better-known works. Blushing on her way out of the kitchen, she surreptitiously helped herself to a forkful of cheesecake.

Twenty-three

It's such a lovely piece of music; perhaps no one would notice, thought Lucinda as the last notes of her favourite string quartet faded.

The late afternoon sun glinted on the open windows and the orange curtains billowed in the breeze. The fragrant summer air filled the café. She glanced at the patrons, who didn't look as if they were going to budge. Some were sipping at their coffees that certainly must have long turned cold. Would you like me to warm that up for you, madam? Cynical thoughts started to brew in her mind. Why do some people even bother to go to cafés, especially if they just come to stare at their laptops?

Dismayed she flicked through the owner's CDs, resigning herself to the fact that she'd have to play something else after all. Borodin? Never heard of him. Suk? Fibich? All unknown to her. Well it was never too late to learn, she thought, realising that waitressing could do wonders in filling the gaps in her knowledge of classical music. In the meantime, though, she again flirted with the idea of playing the same music again. No one's going to notice, she reassured herself, and took a chance and pressed the play button whilst giving the guests a quick look, but they seemed blissfully unaware of the world around them. In fact, she liked Foerster's *String Quartet No.4* so much that she would sometimes play it several times, always hoping the guests would leave before the last of the three movements was over. Upon hearing the opening notes of the *Allegro grazioso*, she was able to put on her most cheerful expression whenever she met someone's eyes.

Not only were the same people still glued to their seats, more customers seemed to be entering the café. Lucinda resigned herself to the fact that it was going to be a busy Saturday. Everyone seems to gravitate to this café, Lucinda pondered. But why? Hidden in a small alley, it was rather a bit off the beaten track. They're probably all attracted to its 1930s charm. Everything about the place was aesthetic and welcoming, even if you felt you were sitting in your grandparents' living room. Although, I don't think Irma would approve of chairs that didn't match or a red-velvet settee, for that matter. I wonder what her house was like; perhaps she even had such a drawing room with huge mirrors and imposing lampshades. Come to think of it, I wish my living room looked like this! Perhaps I could paint it one day. She made a point of going to buy some brushes and paint soon.

In the short time she had been in Brno, Lucinda had learned how to fuse her waitressing tasks and her rampant thoughts without becoming lost in excessive day-dreaming. This behaviour, though, often made her forget dates and other appointments she had made, such as the one she had with a certain Mr Strouhanka shortly after her shift that day.

Twenty-four

"Has anyone ever painted you?" Eric wanted to know.

"Well, not long ago Dorothy and I posed for each other a few times," Sarah answered.

"She's the one..." he began.

"...whose work you recently admired at our exhibition," Sarah interrupted, before rolling her eyes to one side and managing an ironic smile.

"And how did you paint one another?" he continued keenly.

"Oh, it was merely a matter of having a figure in the background devoid of any realistic details," Sarah said, looking at Eric as if awaiting another question. Let him make an effort, she thought to herself playfully. A silence ensued.

"Interestingly enough, the critics have claimed that you couldn't be pigeonholed," Eric said, before giving Sarah an enquiring look.

"Well, that's a change from all the gruesome things they usually write about me and my work."

"How do you react to that?" asked Eric, hoping not just to appease his curiosity but also to keep the communication flowing between them. They had decided to have a picnic at Maroondah Dam near her grandparents' place. "I imagine it must be disheartening to read negative things about one's work. I know I'd be spluttering with rage!"

"In the beginning I was livid. I actually wanted to go see them personally to let them know what I thought of their opinions. Though I rarely take anything they write seriously nowadays," Sarah replied.

Not having made up their mind about where to sit down, Sarah and Eric seemed to be walking around in circles.

"They probably help you see your work in another light," Eric said in a consolatory tone as they came to the main picnic area with the overwhelmingly large dam walls in the background.

"True, but what surprises me most is how they all seem to be drunk on their own thoughts as they conjure up statements that have more to do with psychoanalysis than art," Sarah added.

"Why can't they just write normally?" Eric asked as they both suddenly stopped in front of a huge sundial surrounded by Roman numerals embedded in the grass.

"Then they wouldn't be art critics, would they? Anyway, you can't imagine the number of times I've had to look up some of the words they use. Nothing but erudite gibberish, if you ask me!" she concluded.

"They probably studied hard at university for many years to be just like that," he rationalised. "So you can't blame them."

"All they really want to do is cause a stir. Still, a review is a review; good or bad, it inevitably draws attention to one's work," Sarah conceded as they walked around the Roman numerals, appreciating them from different angles.

"I would never have thought of it like that, but you're right. What kind of things do they write?"

"Not long ago one critic described a painting that I had actually sold for an exorbitant sum as being a *miasma of morbidity* of all things. You do get well-wishers, though, who simply praise the artistic aspects of your work." She paused in reflection. "They even have their favourite expressions like 'it's resplendent with this or that quality,' for example." Sarah then turned her attention to the sundial again. "I wonder if we'll get any sun today to get a proper reading?"

"Well, it is rather cloudy; don't know why I bothered bringing my sunglasses. Anyway, what was that painting all about?" he persisted, more intrigued with the artist herself than with the historical sundial.

"It was very dreamlike, and my critic was really going over it with a fine-tooth comb, coming up with all sorts of childhood traumas I must have gone through. Do you think my mind is plagued by incurable neurosis?"

"Is that what he wrote?"

"Well, that's what he implied."

"In any case, we're all neurotic in one way or another. It's what makes us interesting and different from others," he added.

"Why couldn't he have put it so nicely?"

"It was probably his own personal issues getting the better of him. His criticism had nothing to do with you."

"Well, I'm sure he knows his onions in the world of fine arts, which was why I was so thrown when he became so obnoxious. But maybe it was his review that made people curious enough to want to see for themselves," she surmised.

"Then you should actually be grateful to him. That hatchet job may have helped pave the way for the painting's success in the end," Eric figured. "Why did you decide to paint it in the first place, Sarah?"

"It was for a friend who needed a painting as part of a backdrop for a play. His mind was overflowing with ideas. He wanted a 'cubist jungle filled with subtle eroticism amidst an explosion of pastel colours' or something along those lines."

"That was some acrobatic task he set you."

"That was the easy part; he also wanted the painting to evoke certain feelings such as jealousy and rapture, all whilst depicting both life's joys and harsh realities."

"So in actual fact, the critic was unknowingly analysing your friend and his convoluted ideas."

"Well, I'm the one who dabs on the paint, so I do take part of the blame for this eclectic venture."

More clouds seemed to be gathering above them, ending all hope of any sunshine.

"I wonder how this thing works," said Eric as his attention again strayed to the large Roman numerals.

"All I have understood from this sundial is that it's probably going to rain soon. Shall we climb those steps before the heavens open?" she suggested whilst pointing to the path that led to the top of the dam. Feeling peckish, she started to tear off bits of the baguette that was sticking out of their picnic basket. "I can't wait to try those cheeses and that wine you've brought along," she said as she munched away.

The two made their way up the steps. Various lush plants adorned the path until they reached a rotunda about two thirds of the way up. They sat on the bench inside the romantic shelter as raindrops started to patter on the roof. A nervous silence followed.

"Oh, I've forgotten the um…" Before Sarah could articulate the last two syllables, Eric had leaned over and kissed her. Two more long kisses followed.

"What have you forgotten?" Eric asked, taking one of her hands in his, but she just drew him towards her and they kissed for what must have seemed like hours. Sarah extended her free hand to see if the rain had subsided. During such moments, time would lose all significance to her. Intermittent showers were interrupted by brief torrential downpours.

"We're going to have to stay here for a little while," she declared, brimming with delight.

"Why don't we have our picnic here before our stomachs start to growl?" suggested Eric while he took out the cheese, the wine, napkins, knives and two glasses.

"And before I devour the whole baguette!" She blurred her eyes. Had she brought her brushes and easel with her, she would have set them up there and then. For Sarah, art always came first; romance had always been subconsciously relegated to a mere delightful distraction.

Eric poured the wine, then kissed her once again. And again…

"It's just like a dream," she whispered as she opened her eyes.

Just like a dream, Sarah thought to herself. And as soon as she felt her blanket and pillow, the horrible realisation came that it *had* only been a dream. Seeing the familiar features of her bedroom angered her at first. But she had never had such a vivid dream before, so she did her utmost to mentally go through as many details as she could remember before it was all lost forever. I have to keep these thoughts in my mind, so that they will eventually come true in my life. I'll never get anything done if I continue these bad sleeping habits of mine.

After a hearty breakfast, Sarah decided to visit the National Gallery.

Twenty-five

"Terribly sorry I'm late; I didn't notice the time, Mr Strouhanka," Lucinda said apologetically.

"That's okay, I had to take care of some odds and ends around the place anyway. Please come this way."

Lucinda followed the landlord up the four flights of stairs, and eagerly listened to him explain every detail about the interior of the flat on the top floor. It took about half an hour for Lucinda to make up her mind.

"Well this place seems eminently suitable; I think I'll take it," she announced brightly.

"Are you sure? I mean I'll be glad to have you as a tenant, but most people prefer to at least sleep over such a decision before committing themselves. I've had people in the past who didn't think twice about signing the contract, only to end up changing their minds the very next day."

"You needn't worry about me, Mr Strouhanka, I'm definitely sure about this place; it's so charming, and it's not far from town, either."

"Yes, it does have a few things going for it," he said in agreement. "Just look at those magnificent art-deco ceilings, for instance!" he said, pointing to the ornamental designs high above them. "You won't find craftsmanship like that any more."

"Very palatial," she agreed. "But how does one go about changing the light bulbs?" she asked.

"You'll need a ladder for that. There's one in the cellar," he said reassuringly.

"It must be a very long one. How high are the ceilings anyway?"

"Oh, about three and a half metres, I'd say."

"It looks more like four to me."

"That was normal at the end of the nineteenth century when these houses were built. Only aristocratic families lived on Tivoligasse as this street used to be called back then. If only these walls could talk, I'm sure they could tell us a tale or two."

"Well, I don't really want to know, to tell you the truth," Lucinda began. "But I'm sure the good people could at least afford to pay their heating bills. I imagine it must be quite expensive in winter. I mean, it does get cold in this country."

"Probably not much colder than in Britain," the landlord said before opening one of the bay windows to show Lucinda the impressive array of houses on the opposite side.

"Oh my, the trams are a bit loud, aren't they?"

"Oh, you'll get used to them. Everyone does. They run every eight minutes in both directions to and from town. It's very convenient. Just think, you'll never be late again!" he said, smiling.

"Hmm…"

"Look, why don't you think it over?" he suggested as he closed the window. "I'll give you till the middle of the week. No one else is going to look at the flat until then anyway. Alright?"

"That's very kind of you, but I think I'll sign right now," Lucinda said, walking around the large living room and soaking up the atmosphere. "You see, I've been staying with friends of mine since my arrival in Brno, and I wouldn't want to outstay my welcome; I've already abused quite enough of their hospitality. Besides, your flat is partially furnished, which is exactly what I'm looking for."

"Well, it's not very fancy, mind you. It all belonged to my grandparents, so it's somewhat outdated. Some are even antiques from the forties and fifties. Still, everything is working as it's meant to," he declared. They entered another room, but when he tried the switch, one of the lamps failed to light up. "Well, it had been working before the last tenant moved out," he grumbled. "It's probably just the light bulb. I'll have it changed before you move in," he promised.

"Please do. It'll save me the climb."

"Okay, it's three months' notice should you want to move out. No pets, no loud parties..."

"I'm not the partying kind of girl, Mr Strouhanka," she said as if he had just accused her of being one.

"I mention it anyway, as most of the other tenants are pensioners who enjoy the peace and quiet. A few of them are quite hard of hearing, but it still needs to be said," he continued, suddenly exuding an air of authority. Lucinda nodded understandingly.

They went through all the formalities, signing whatever was necessary. Mr Strouhanka appeared to be the kind of person who would just as readily tear up the contract, should Lucinda change her mind in the meantime. However, it was highly unlikely, for ideas were already teeming in her mind as to how she was going to decorate the place. Not that there was really much to change apart from adding the odd picture or two and some curtains, she thought. The place could certainly do with some dusting...

Twenty-six

The late August sun was already shining brightly into Sarah's bedroom. She hurried to switch on the computer and began writing...

From: sarahhafner@arts-stud.melbuni.com.au
Sent: Monday, 24.08.2015, 16:02
To: Mr Thaunton
Re: overwhelmed!

Dear Mr Thaunton,

Seeing that all traces of my sinister flu had disappeared, I decided to go and see the Australian impressionism collection at the National Gallery this afternoon. I have to admit that I thoroughly enjoyed not only being able to recognise some of the works we had already discussed in class, but also seeing the originals. I didn't expect them to have such a profound effect on my emotions, though. At first I marvelled at what the artists were able to produce back then, but when I came to a corner devoted to several of Charles Conder's paintings, I literally wept. It's true! I must have been a sight to those who happened to notice me. They probably thought that something terrible had just happened. There I was, sobbing as I gazed at two of his masterpieces. I then quickly focussed my attention on some of the other works to distract myself and to regain some composure. I returned one more time to try to properly appreciate the paintings, but as soon as I got close enough, I simply couldn't hold back the tears for some reason. Have you ever experienced something like that before? It was quite silly of me, for I'm not usually like that at all, so it's definitely the painter's fault. Or perhaps it's because I also paint, which makes me vulnerable in some way.

I thought I'd share this emotional account with you first, and give the others a more rational version in class tomorrow, although it would be interesting to see if any other students had similar reactions.

Yours,
Sarah Hafner

From: thaunton@arts-fac.melbuni.com.au
Sent: Monday, 24.08.2015, 20:28
To: Sarah Hafner
Re: involuntary reactions

Dear Sarah,

I suppose your reaction is not uncommon for an artist. You probably perceived something in the paintings that struck a sensitive chord within you. Or it could be the realisation that paintings will eventually survive their creators. Some people also experience something called the *Stendhal syndrome*, so don't worry, you're not the only one to be overwhelmed by a work of art.

I'll have to make a point of taking a closer look at

those particular paintings when I go there next time. I'm all curious now!

What kinds of things do you paint by the way?

See you in class tomorrow,
Thaunton

Twenty-seven

About three months after arriving in Brno, Lucinda started going out with a photographer called Karel, whom she had met at a gallery one day. On a whim, she had decided to visit an exhibition of the photographs and films made by an adventurer called Eduard Ingriš. He had also been a composer and a conductor before the Second World War. Fearing the aftermath of the communist putsch in Czechoslovakia, he left his native country and travelled to Peru, where he conducted the Lima Symphony Orchestra. In need of yet further exploits, he and two fellow compatriots not only set out on several expeditions through the rainforests of the Amazon, but also embarked on two perilous sea voyages, which subsequently became the feature of an incredible documentary film. His name would have faded into total obscurity, had it not been for one of his fellow seafarer's initiatives to bring his photographic and film archives back to his homeland. Seeing this exhibition made Lucinda aware of the possibility of sliding into obscurity herself.

The gallery was rather crowded that day, so she obediently followed the masses, allocating the same amount of time to each picture as the person before her. Yet she felt she was only looking at them superficially. About halfway, though, she suddenly stood motionless between two photographs. One depicted a locomotive half buried in rubble near a place called Matucana, the other showed two men that were trying to tie a coffin onto a donkey. For some reason she couldn't go on. The queue of people behind her simply made their way around her without giving these two photographs any special attention.

On his way back round the exhibition of photographs, Karel noticed the faraway gaze of the young woman who had already caught his eye when he had entered the building. He had two choices. He could simply continue with his perusal of the remaining pictures and forget all about the woman, thereby forgoing his only chance of ever being able to meet her, or he could go up to this intriguing stranger to find out who she was. He had often found himself in such a situation, not really knowing what he was supposed to do. Should he ignore her and just appreciate the fact that such an enchanting being had appeared in his life for a few moments? After all, he soon had an appointment to keep with a client who needed some portraits taken. Yet wouldn't he regret not having at least tried to make contact with her? On the other hand, perhaps he would be doing himself a psychological favour if he ignored her, he mused as he thought about a few girlfriends he would rather not have met in his life, but ended up getting to know on account of his impulsive nature. However, this time he experienced such a gut-wrenching feeling that simply couldn't be shrugged off. She could have made it easier for him by walking away or getting lost amongst the crowd. But she just stood there staring at the same two photographs without budging.

"Oh, excuse me, I'm terribly sorry," said a man as he bumped into Karel, who had also ceased to move only ten metres away from where Lucinda was standing.

"That's alright," he replied, taken aback that someone could be so prodigiously polite in this country. Then without knowing exactly how, he went straight up to Lucinda and stood next to her for a while before he thought the moment was right to turn to her and smile.

"It's incredible, isn't it?" Karel couldn't think of anything else to say. In his mind, though, he wasn't referring to the subject matter in the photographs.

"Indeed," she said spontaneously. "Anyway, I think you've just saved me, for I can't seem to stop looking at them."

"Perhaps it wasn't the best idea to place these two next to each other," Karel suggested.

"It makes everything seem so futile, so pointless. It most likely took years for this poor country to be able to buy a locomotive, and for some reason it plummeted into this gorge and has probably been rusting away there ever since."

"It makes you wonder what happened to the rest of the train," said Karel, now also absorbed by the photo that hadn't aroused so much speculation the first time he saw it.

"Imagine if the artist himself had travelled on this very train," she reflected. "Had he been in the wrong place at the wrong time, he would neither have produced such photographs nor accomplished his other remarkable feats."

"And if he had actually plunged to his death back in 1949, we wouldn't be here now talking to each other."

"That's true," she said, not taking her eyes off the second photograph. "Yet at times it's hard to understand what cruel fate life dishes up for some people," she went on, before briefly looking at Karel. "Like the person who ended up in this coffin or the poor donkey that has to carry the whole burden." The scenario made her somehow think of Blanka and Irma.

"Who would have thought that a day at the gallery could turn out to be such a philosophical experience," he said as their eyes met.

"We should be grateful to Mr Ingriš and whoever had

the idea of putting on this exhibition," she said, still deep in thought.

"But wait, perhaps it's not at all what we think," Karel said all of a sudden.

"What do you mean?"

"You still haven't seen the rest of the photographs, have you?"

"Well no, not yet." Karel sensed that he was slowly succeeding in riveting her attention away from these two photographs.

"You see, the man not only worked as a photographer but also as a cameraman for a number of film companies, where he even had the privilege of working with Hemingway. There are a few photos of the two posing together."

"I don't understand."

"I'm just speculating, but this locomotive could have been a part of a scene in one of his movies."

"As I said, you have come to save me from my negative visions," she declared. "I'm Lucinda, by the way," she said, extending her hand that Karel simply held rather than shake.

"Extremely pleased to meet you. Now this whole collection has entranced me in more ways than one… Um, my name's Karel, and I would love to continue our conversation at Kavárna Podnebi, which is a nice café not far from here."

"Why not! I'd love to," she replied. "Just like everything else in life, it was simply meant to be."

"Please keep talking, I love your accent," he said.

"Oh do stop, I'm probably blushing all over!"

As the courtyard of the café was already filled with students from the nearby faculty of music, Lucinda and Karel had to content themselves with a quiet table inside, where they spent a delightful hour chatting about their lives. Karel had consequently lost all track of time and was going to be unforgivably late for his meeting. Yet he just couldn't tear himself away from the woman who had mesmerized him and who was now revealing so much about herself.

Twenty-eight

I'm usually so tongue-tied when it comes to speaking about myself, lamented Sarah. She began nervously picking at the dry skin next to her finger nails on both thumbs. For about half an hour she stared alternately at her computer screen and through the window, mulling over what she was going to say to Mr Thaunton. Over a week had passed since they last mailed. Nothing ever seems right to us self-conscious beings, as we always tend to be plagued with thoughts of sounding too ordinary. Once she became aware of her aching thumbs, she urged herself to simply type the first thing that occurred to her. And just when I thought I had kicked that dreadful habit, she complained. She smeared the affected areas with Savlon. I could at least begin by telling him why it has taken so long to reply...

> From: sarahhafner@arts-stud.melbuni.com.au
> Sent: Tuesday, 01.09.2015, 22:46
> To: Mr Thaunton
> Re: what I like to paint
>
> Dear Mr Thaunton,
>
> Wanting to read up on some more Heidelberg School painters over a week ago, I began googling the term, but

my computer crashed! The old dinosaur had obviously reached its date of planned obsolescence, and I had to go out and buy a new one. This is why I wasn't able to write back earlier. Anyway, I went down to my local library and within ten minutes I had all the books I really needed on the subject. It was fascinating, yet I didn't experience the same unexpected reaction when I saw the paintings again in the books. So it definitely had something to do with the originals.

My father was burning the midnight oil the last few nights, installing programs and getting everything running again, and thanks to him, I'm connected once more. Funny how we're so dependent on these contraptions. I somehow don't belong to this generation. Do you ever feel that way?

Today's lesson was a real eye-opener! It's astounding how different interpretations of the same paintings can be. I guess most people just project aspects of their own lives onto the art works. I've seen the painting Dorothy showed you. I don't know if she mentioned it to you, but she's also a keen painter herself. As for me, I like to paint impressionist landscapes and abstracts with a subtle touch of fauvism thrown in just to confuse everyone!

As to the topic of my paper, I'd like to write about Clarice Beckett, who lived entirely for her art. Just seems so unfair that her work wasn't appreciated until forty years after her death. I wonder how she felt about her own generation?

Anyway, wishing you a lovely week.

Yours,
Sarah Hafner

A few seconds after pressing the *send* button, she was already regretting her choice of words. He'll now probably think I'm too pretentious, she instantly thought, and then started to ruminate on what she could have written instead. Well, I can't turn back the clock and change it, can I? And even if I could, there's no guarantee that his reaction would be any different or better. Why does everything have to be so complicated?

Twenty-nine

"It's as easy as falling off a log! Look, I'll show you. After making sure the fuse is out or that the light is definitely switched off, you connect the wires: brown to brown, and blue to blue. Actually with those two wires, it doesn't really matter even if you connect brown to blue," Karel explained.

"That looks simple enough, but what about that green and yellow striped wire that's hanging there?"

"Oh just ignore that one."

"You sure it won't zap electricity in all directions and set fire to the place?" Lucinda's face reflected her anxiety.

"There's really nothing to worry about. But if it'll make you feel better, I'll cable it off for you."

"Yes, please do. I'm so glad you're here to help me. I tend to get all paranoid about invisible things like currents."

"Sure. Actually all this work makes you thirsty. Feel like a beer?" Karel asked as he went into the kitchen.

"Good idea, it'll calm me down," she called after him.

"So tell me more about this diary you've been reading," Karel said as he returned with two bottles of beer.

"I'm only about a third of the way through it, but it is rather compelling," Lucinda said excitedly. "Cheers!"

"Yeah, it must be very eye-opening to read about the

ordeals your grandmother went through," Karel agreed as he sipped his beer.

"I grew up in England so I can't relate to them as much as you probably can. And having known Irma since I was a child also makes it incredibly hard to imagine her the way she actually was. The woman took so many risks! She's lucky she didn't end up like her cellmate Blanka, whom I told you about last time. I see her in a new light now."

Thirty

I had only been out of prison for a month, and was just settling down to the insignificance of life on our collective farm, with its dull administrative work. But then I received a letter without a postage stamp on it. At first I thought it quite odd for someone to deliver a letter personally, when they could simply have knocked at the door. But perhaps they didn't want to arouse any suspicion or alarm anyone. People can be rather callous these days and very likely to inform on their own neighbours if they see something out of the ordinary. I popped it into my bag on my way to the local shops in Rousínov, but couldn't stop thinking about it. Normally letters are censored and once approved, delivered a week or so later, or not at all, depending on their contents.

I couldn't help but look over my shoulder every few minutes, but finally I decided that everything that looked suspicious to me was probably just an ordinary street scene. So I thought it best to simply act inconspicuously. Must try to look miserable and frown a lot like everybody else. They should call it 'gloomism' instead of communism, she reflected. I'll just pretend I'd been queuing for hours to buy some bananas.

Though I was tired from the long walk, on my way back from the shops I decided to go as far as the stream to read the mysterious letter. Nobody would suspect me of getting up to anything dubious there, would they?

Brno, 8th April, 1953

Dear Irma,

I need to see you, it's about Blanka. Please come to one of my classes on the third floor of the natural science faculty off Leninova Street. I teach English there Mondays to Thursdays from four till six in the evening.

Kind regards,
Colin Wood

Well, so much for my uneventful existence, thought Irma. I can't imagine why the secret police haven't stormed the British Council by now after Blanka's testimony. Or maybe they're condoning it on purpose, as it gives them first-hand information on who's likely to be an undercover spy. Czech spies probably enrol in courses themselves as a counter move.

When she finally summoned up the courage to visit this mysterious Colin, who had contacted her out of the blue, she had to think of a way of getting there. The current agricultural fair, which hardly anyone from her collective seemed willing to attend, provided her with a plausible excuse to go to Brno. And Honza, who she knew from another collective farm, was not only obliged to represent the village, but, more importantly, he was the only person privileged to own a car.

During the drive to Brno a week later, he constantly moaned about the fair being nothing more than a host of organised speeches made by various representatives from all over the country and other member states of the Eastern bloc.

"What they won't mention, Irma," he went on, "is that productivity has plummeted, and soon they'll have to subsidize all the cooperatives if we're to survive at all! It's a good thing most of us village folk had saved up for a rainy day during all those years of opulence before the war."

"I think that rain will soon turn into a deluge that will last for decades," lamented Irma. "Many even say that there's going to be a radical currency reform, which will basically wipe out those savings," she said, alluding to what Blanka had revealed to her secretly behind bars.

"They wouldn't do that," he began, "I mean, I wouldn't put anything past this mob, but surely it will never come to that," he said as he parked his Škoda 1200 near the fairgrounds.

"Well, whatever you do, don't go hiding all that money you've saved under your bed," she warned as they got out of the car.

As Honza had dreaded, the fair had been a series of speeches not only glorifying collectivization but also promulgating utopian five-year plans and, of course, denouncing the enemies of Marxism. Okay, been there, done that, thought Irma as they regurgitated the phrases she read daily in the newspapers. Unnoticed, she sidled towards the exit doors and silently made her escape. It was high time, too, seeing it was already past five o'clock. She caught a tram heading towards the quarter of Veveří and got off at Leninova Street. She found the building, and a kind lady directed her to Colin's class. Before she could knock, the door flew open, and several participants slowly made their way out. After the last student passed her, she looked into the room.

"Sorry to interrupt," she said cautiously.

"Please come in. Are you a new student?"

"Well no, actually, I'm Irma, the one you sent the letter to," she said, sounding fraught.

"Of course," he managed to say, his mien suddenly changing. "Pleased to meet you," he said smiling. "Colin

Wood." They shook hands. "I'm glad you could make it," he said as he discreetly scrutinized her.

"Well, it wasn't easy. You see, I'm meant to be representing our village at the trade fair, but I managed to get away," she said uneasily.

"Well, let's not waste any more time then. I suggest we go some place where we won't be disturbed. We have reason to believe that our classrooms are being bugged," he whispered.

"All because of Blanka?" she asked.

"Shh! Keep your voice down," he urged, and led her into the hall. "It's probably just a precautionary measure the State takes wherever foreigners are based," he explained. "So I suggest we go somewhere inconspicuous such as up to Špilberk Castle," he proposed.

"Good idea!" Irma agreed. "No one would ever suspect two people walking around there, would they?"

"Well, we'll just have to pretend we're a young couple making wedding plans, for instance. Let's find you some flowers first," Colin added. On their way out, he took the flowers out of a vase from the reception area and wrapped them in paper. "There, that should do it. Um…for you," he said as charmingly as he could. Irma started to relax.

"Thank you," Irma replied, and played along as if it were a game. She liked his playful manner.

Without beating about the bush, Colin explained to me that he had found out about my friendship with Blanka from a fellow agent, and that my life was in danger since I apparently knew too much. This is where Colin started to show his serious side. Once Blanka had let on about the Czechs having succeeded in planting a mole in the British Cabinet, possibly even a minister, it was all-out panic stations. I would never have guessed that thanks to Blanka, I was also at the centre of their investigations. The British were desperate to conceal this information at all costs, and unless I cooperated, well, he told me, there would be dire consequences. Instead of becoming overanxious, I started to fall under his dominating spell; his alluring gaze and his words were literally mesmerizing me. There was also something about this man's nature that made me trust him and so I told him everything I knew. To do otherwise would have been very foolish indeed, as one wrong word or a display of unreasonable behaviour, and I could have ended up like Blanka. Colin also informed me that a fellow agent had tried to negotiate a deal with her, but she foolishly turned out to be rather recalcitrant, even going so far as reporting the matter to the authorities, which she believed would earn her a reprieve. Even traitors deserved a second chance, she naively thought, but unfortunately for her, the Czech secret service (also known as the STB) became suspicious, and Colin even suspects they organised a wet job on her while she was still in prison.

It was Colin's task to extract as much information out of me as he possibly could, which wasn't very difficult, seeing that I had no qualms about telling him everything I knew. I mean, how could I be loyal to the crooks that had given democracy a whole new meaning? Personally, they had not just taken away most of our property, but they had also ruined my brother's career and made me spend a year in jail for being a so-called *counter-revolutionary*. Well, I thought there and then, now's the time to start living up to my new title. 'God save the King!' I said to Colin as we drank a beer together at a small pub after our little stroll through the gardens of Špilberk Castle. Apparently, though, the monarch had died the year before and now a queen reigned over Britain. Well, news like that simply didn't spread in Czech prisons I told an astonished Colin. We started to speak about more general things. Although he spoke openly about his upbringing as well as his interest in Slavic languages and Czech classical music, he wasn't too eager to reveal anything else. I in turn told him so much about myself, including the trials and tribulations I'd been through that he slowly began to trust me. I promised to translate my diary for him, which contained all the confidential information Blanka had shared with me. He accompanied me to the central bus station and bought me a ticket for the last bus. We arranged to meet the following week at the reservoir. Before I boarded the bus, he took my hand and squeezed it lightly.

All the while I asked myself what it was about Colin that attracted me so much. No other man had ever had such an effect on me. I sighed as the bus pulled noisily out of the dreary station. Even Colin couldn't help but remark that he had never seen a more depressing place in his life. He waved as he stood there on the pavement, seeing me off. It wasn't long before I realised that it must be the element of danger and rebellion involved that excited me. Rather than panic, I relished the risks I was taking. In a way I saw it as a vengeance for the things we'd had to endure. I was intent on cooperating and working all the more ardently, knowing that if I did so, I would become part of a whole new world, wherever it would lead me. Forty minutes later I was back in my sleepy town again. I got off the old bus and watched it rattle away into the distance. Anxious thoughts suddenly filled my mind. My attention then turned to all the moths surging towards the street lamp above me. If they get too close to the intense heat of the glowing lamp, they will burn to death, but by cautiously flying around its contours, they only risk having their wings slightly singed. Some humans are perversely attracted to things that could bring about their demise, yet, instead of trying to free themselves, they cling to the ominous circumstances, possibly enjoying the thrill of it all. Perhaps that's a sign that I mustn't become too involved with Colin. Knowing that it could all come to an abrupt end made me decide to simply take each day as it came. For all I knew, Colin might vanish into thin air once he had all the information he needed. Yet I cared little of what was to become of me in such an eventuality – even if it meant spending the rest of my days on the farm. Although somehow I couldn't see that happening. I decided under that street lamp there and then that I was one moth that was going to play her cards right. In the meantime, however, it was off to bed for me.

Thirty-one

That night Lucinda tossed and turned in her sleep. Just as she thought about getting up and making herself a cup of linden tea, she finally fell soundly asleep.

It was three o'clock in the morning. Karel had just immortalised Lucinda in a photograph he had enlarged after their night of intense love-making. After hanging up the photo to dry, he left the dark room and made his way upstairs to bed. It wasn't long before he was sound asleep. Lucinda nestled into her new lover's arms, envious of his ability to switch off on command while the day's worries still whirled around in her own mind. She stared at him sleeping peacefully at her side. Her attention then turned to her hormones, and she wondered what she would do if she fell pregnant. She knew that her ovulation period was still a few days away, and her charts on the moon phases had never let her down, so it was highly unlikely this time. She was nevertheless worried, and her thoughts obviously weren't intent on sparing her nerves that night. Although she lay there long enough to witness the room slowly fill with light as a new day started to emerge, she finally fell asleep with the soothing sound of the chirping birds outside. She awoke to the smell of coffee and fresh pastries that her lover had bought from a corner bakery.

"They only had pastries with sweet walnut filling at this

time of morning," he said as he brought in their breakfast. Lucinda took a look at the clock and was startled to see both hands facing north.

"It's late!"

"That's all they had left, I'm afraid."

"No, that's fine," she said as she took a generous bite out of one. "Delicious," she munched. "You'll probably forget all about me when you're big and famous one day," she said without looking at him.

"And when your singing career takes off, who's going to forget whom?" he retorted.

"If anyone's going to make the big time here, it's you and your group of fellow avant-garde photographers."

"It's not any particular kind of art that makes you famous, dearest one, but who you know."

"I guess you're right," Lucinda concluded while she stretched and yawned. Then she suddenly noticed that the lamp above the bed had become loose and was about to fall on top of them. "Look out!" she screamed.

"What's wrong? What is it?" Karel asked alarmed in half sleep.

"The lamp!" Lucinda looked up towards the ceiling only to see the lamp hanging motionlessly above them.

"What about the lamp?"

"Oh, thank God for that! It's still there."

"Where else would it be; we secured it to the ceiling yesterday," Karel said to remind her.

"Sorry, I just had this crazy dream...oh never mind." She kissed him and smiled. "Good morning. Would you be an angel and go fetch us some croissants from the bakery across the road?"

"Sure, just let me wake up properly first," he said without making any effort to actually get out of bed. He turned to look at the alarm clock ticking quietly under the bed. "It's late, Lucinda. I doubt if they'll have any left at this time," he said, and raised himself, but slowly crept back under the sheets. "Mmh, I feel like doing other things right now."

"Cheeky," she replied and started to writhe lasciviously.

Karel proceeded to rip off her pyjama top and gently kiss her breasts, before making his way downward.

"Mm, your hands are nice and warm this time," she said in approval as she pulled off her pyjama bottoms under the sheets.

Despite not having slept as much as Karel, she found she was full of energy. She turned around and was soon on top of him, and began to wrap her legs tightly around his waist.

"Now, you can't move and you're all mine for the taking!"

Karel willingly succumbed every time to Lucinda's rampant sexual nature and let her do as she pleased. When Lucinda was passionately aroused, nothing else seemed to matter to her.

"You only care about gratifying your carnal needs, don't you?" Karel teased her.

"Mmh. I'm catching up, as I've had a lot of withdrawal symptoms all these years. Anyway, I'll be off to see an aunt up in the country this weekend, so I won't see you until next Monday," she explained, but all thoughts soon gave way to the tingling sensations that pervaded their bodies. Once Lucinda felt exhaustion taking over, she twisted her body in such a way as to allow Karel to enter her as deeply as possible to heighten their level of rapture.

"Push now! Oh yes, let's come together," she moaned blissfully. They quivered in voluptuous delight and both just lay there without moving a muscle.

"That's the best way to greet the day," Lucinda said snuggling up to Karel.

"You won't believe what the time is," Karel said, after counting the chimes that resounded from outside.

Thirty-two

The university clock struck a quarter to five, but according to Mr Thaunton's 1964 Accurist wrist watch – a rare gem he had managed to buy on eBay after outbidding several other potential buyers, it was five to five in the afternoon. It wasn't running fast, on the contrary, the watch was in perfect order despite its age. He just liked to set it ten minutes ahead of the actual time to curb his old habit of being chronically late, even for his own lectures.

It was the last day of semester and also the deadline for submitting a 5,000-word assignment on the style of an unconventional painter of the students' choice. The number of papers in his pigeonhole had been accumulating the whole day, for most of his students were in the habit of leaving everything till the last minute. He took out the thick pile and plonked it onto his desk, wondering whether he should have a quick glance at Sarah's. He then decided against it, as he still needed to post his proposal for a conference he wanted to attend in Germany next February. It wasn't only a way of furthering his academic career, he was also keen to escape another scorching hot summer. A glance at his prized watch made him quicken his pace. 5pm, which meant he had ten more minutes before the post office closed for the day. He straightened the papers and placed them in his leather bag with a sigh as he thought about the long hours he would need to correct them all. The prospect of not being able to see Sarah every week also disheartened him. It occurred to him that they had not exchanged any emails for over a month. Oh well, he thought, girls like her normally have either boyfriends or lots of other things to do with their time rather than being infatuated with their teachers. Anyway, I had better concentrate on finishing my paper in case I am accepted.

Seeing that such conferences were few and far between, Thaunton made it a habit to apply even if the topic of his paper was only remotely related to the theme of the conference in question. After all, it wasn't just about securing a much-coveted academic grant, it was also about getting one's work published. He had his heart set on this particular conference in Heidelberg, as it primarily dealt with the impact of impressionism around the world. He presumed that they would jump at the opportunity of having someone talk about Australian impressionism, provided no one else beat him to it, of course. It would be the perfect follow-up to a series of lectures he would be giving at Masaryk University in Brno just prior to the conference date. He had actually been hoping to go to Charles University in Prague, yet they already seemed to be inundated with applicants wanting to do the same. But then again, he thought, at least they were kind enough to refer me to Brno.

The long queue slowly slithered inside the post office. The woman in front of Thaunton sneezed several times. As if that wasn't enough, the man behind him started incessantly blowing his nose. Not a good time to be breathing, he thought to himself.

Sarah was the first to leave the lecture hall. Her class had gone on longer than usual, so she dashed through the French department before making her determined way down the steps of her building. Five to five, I could still make it, she encouraged herself as she hurriedly crossed the campus heading towards the Old Arts building. Up the stairs, third office on the right. Knock! Knock! No answer. Bother! I think I just blew my chance of being able to chat with my favourite teacher, she silently lamented. She caught sight of another student from her class, who was also looking for some sign of life at the other end of the corridor. Shaking his head and muttering something less than flattering, he turned around and began walking in Sarah's direction.

"He's already left his office and it isn't even five o'clock yet!" the student grumbled. Suddenly the clock outside struck five times.

"Well it is now!" she said to the student, whose name was Redmond. He was one of those alternative types who always sat in the back row. He played in a band, which was his real passion in life. Flirting also came easily to him. In any case, he always gave the impression that his studies were something of a nuisance that had to be endured, thus preventing an existence of full-time creativity.

"Great! Well…" he shrugged his shoulders, "I guess we could always leave our assignments in his pigeonhole; he's bound to look there sometime next week, or once he realises a few papers are missing," Redmond reasoned in all confidence.

"Good idea, but I think I'll also send him an email…just in case," added Sarah as they made their way to where the faculty pigeonholes were situated. They were then met by two other students who were also eager to part with their essays. While the foursome took turns easing their work into the narrow slot below Mr Thaunton's name, he himself had just left the post office. He was met by a chilly wind, and it hadn't stopped raining, but he didn't let this dampen his spirits. It was Friday, after all, and he was looking forward to a bowl of delicious fettuccine carbonara at *Tiamo's*, which had become a kind of ritual for him ever since his own student days in the nineties. Apart from the fond memories, he somehow trusted a place where you could see Italian mammas cooking in a half-opened kitchen at the back of the restaurant. There was also something comforting about its familiarity, such as the chequerboard floor, the small wooden tables and all the colourful signs and posters on the walls, including a rare old Spencer Street station railway sign. He always wondered how they had managed to procure it. When he arrived, he was quite surprised to find that the place was almost full despite it being nowhere near dinnertime. After surveying the interior, he saw that the only free table was facing the window. He preferred to sit where he had a view of the stairs and the kitchen, as he wasn't fond of watching passers-by on Lygon Street. After some hesitation, he decided to stay nevertheless and therefore not break with tradition. In the meantime, Sarah, Redmond and the other two students had decided to celebrate the end of semester at a nearby pub.

Happily full, Thaunton pushed his bowl aside and finished his glass of wine. He would have loved to order a cappuccino, as the smell of ground coffee hovered enticingly in the air, but he didn't want to risk staying awake half the night, so he opted for a hot chocolate instead. He envied those who could savour frothy coffees all day and still manage to sleep like logs. It's funny how one's mind is swamped with thoughts and images when alone in a public place, he mused, and how disparate they could be.

Must remember to buy some fresh bread in the morning and silver beet for that quiche I want to bake… We're playing against Hawthorn tomorrow, or was it on Sunday? Got so close to winning last time… Should get these corrections out of the way first though... It's still raining and yet there are three clowns outside smoking! I could never be a slave to an addiction or anything... If I hurried, I could still catch the 7:25pm train this evening... 'Ever fallen in love with someone you shouldn't have fallen in love with...' Haven't heard that song in ages! I think I had just started high school when it was in the charts. Pity Sarah didn't drop by my office today; we could have had a nice chat... I wonder if she...

"Here's your hot chocolate, Sir!" said an ever-cheerful waitress.

"Oh, thanks," he replied, and as he looked out of the window again, catching glimpses of countless passers-by, he thought he actually saw his favourite student. A woman who was carrying a bag similar to Sarah's caught his attention, but he wasn't really sure it was her. Perhaps he was only hoping it was Sarah. For a second, he considered going outside to double check, but even if he did search her out of the crowd, what would he say to her? 'The topic of your paper sounds fascinating!' But, he hadn't paid yet, and besides, she would be at least a whole block away from the restaurant by now. It's funny how we long for people we don't know that well yet, Mr Thaunton mused; we do everything we can to entice them into our lives, only to take them for granted once they're actually there. Yet somehow he was sure Sarah was an exception, able to transfix him long after the novelty of their initial magnetism had worn off. While he sipped his hot chocolate, he pulled out all the papers and flicked through them. I could go on a digestive stroll around Lygon Street later, he speculated, more in the hope of bumping into Sarah than anything else. After checking the pile twice, he realised to his surprise that her paper as well as a number of others were missing.

Thirty-three

Colin kept looking out of the classroom window to watch out for Irma. Once he spotted her walking towards the building, he scurried down the stairs and met her in the doorway.

"Hello Colin," Irma said, eyeing him admiringly. She was fond of tweed jackets. She herself was also dressed elegantly.

"Hello Irma, all ready for our little picnic?"

"Ready when you are." Irma beamed, and then looked up to the heavens. "But the weather's not on our side today," she said as scattered raindrops started to fall.

"Did anybody see you?" Colin asked anxiously. He put his arm around her as they made their way towards the tram stop under his umbrella.

"I don't think so. I kept looking back to check if anyone was following me, but nothing looked suspicious. Although in our village there's no escape from prying eyes."

"How do you mean?" Colin asked.

"Well, there's old Miss Hrozná who watches anyone who happens to be waiting for a bus. Her house is directly in front of the stop. She always pretends to be watering the plants. Oh, I think she's quite harmless," Irma went on, "although her poor plants must be thoroughly drenched!"

"You can never be too sure about anyone these days."

"Oh, she's just a retired office worker who lives alone."

"The secret police often prey on bored pensioners, goading them on to inform on their fellow comrades. Former public servants are prime targets for them," he began, "seeing that they have a life-long history of adhering to regulations; it's second nature to them."

"Now that you mention it, she was a trifle too inquisitive today," Irma began uncertainly. "She wanted to know, for example, what business I had in the city that was more important than work."

"What did you tell her?"

"That I had to see a sick aunt, but then she started asking all sorts of questions about her. Do you think she was interrogating me?" Irma asked.

"Hard to say. Next time, tell her you're going to fetch some mandarines and chocolates," Colin suggested.

"There's no way she'd believe that," Irma objected. "Knowing her, she'd want to see them afterwards!"

"Then you'll just have to bring her some," Colin said decisively.

"How will you manage that?" Irma asked, but was somehow sure Colin had a few tricks up his sleeve.

"I'll organise it through the Council. They take good care of us here, you know."

"I'm impressed," Irma said as a tram slowly coasted to a halt at their stop opposite the Botanic Gardens. They boarded the tram and hardly exchanged a word amongst the crowds of people. She eyed the other passengers with suspicion, wondering which one of them was working for the secret police.

After they had arrived at the reservoir, they slowly made their way around the meandering paths along the water's edge. Although nothing seemed out of the ordinary, they wondered whether they were being followed or not, but neither of them noticed anything suspicious, so they assumed the Party had bigger fish to fry that day. If only they knew that state secrets were about to be divulged, thought Irma to herself.

"My shoes are soaked," Irma said, after they had found a secluded bench under a linden tree overlooking the vast expanse of the reservoir. They had walked about five kilometres from the dam walls. "Do you think anyone will find us here?" Irma asked as Colin sat down next to her.

"I think we're quite safe," he said, and took her hand. "Actually, all we have to do to avert attention is pretend we're just an ordinary couple in love and…" He wanted to continue, but before he knew exactly how it happened, he found himself kissing Irma passionately. The two had willingly succumbed to the palpable tension that had gradually been developing between them, so they couldn't have given a better rendition of two lovebirds. After several minutes, Irma sighed and leaned back.

"I apologise, Irma, that wasn't meant to have happened. I hardly know you, yet I seem to have taken advantage of you and…"

"You have my permission to take further advantage of me," she said, urging him to kiss her again. Colin caressed her hands and kissed Irma again, obviously not needing any additional encouragement.

"You have a way of weakening my willpower and…my sense of morality, I'm afraid," he admitted.

"Are British men always so polite and gentlemanly?"

"Well yes, but you also need to be able to read between the lines every now and then," he replied.

"I see," Irma said frivolously before slowly coming to her senses. "Um, before we forget why we're here…" she said, reaching into her bag and taking out several bound pages. "This contains almost everything that Blanka told me in prison, including the names of the three most important spies currently working in the UK, the Party's planned currency reform later this year, and, believe it or not, there's trouble brewing in Australia as well," Irma went on as she handed him the bound sheets.

"Australia!" Colin said in astonishment.

"The Soviets have been using the Czech consulate in Australia for their espionage activities, seeing that it comes under less suspicion than their own embassy," Irma added.

"Now I am impressed," Colin nodded, his eyes widening considerably.

"That's not all! They are also in the process of retraining a couple of Australian diplomats who have shown sympathies to the communist cause," she concluded. "I guess they are trying to expand their empire wherever they can."

"So it appears. Anyhow, I must deliver this information to headquarters as soon as possible, and then await further instructions from my superiors. You do understand, I hope?" he asked her solemnly.

"Of course, do as you must," she said. "Will I ever see you again or is this the end of our game?" she asked, watching the raindrops pelting down.

"Oh, I'll be back in about two weeks at the latest," he replied. "There's still plenty of work for me here."

"What kind of work?" she asked anxiously. "Nothing dangerous, I trust."

"Just banal things really. A colleague and I have to check the eligibility of about a dozen prominent figures wanting to emigrate to the UK, which means we just have to make sure they have no political affiliations with the Party," he explained.

"Oh."

"There are also one or two other activities I'm involved in, but the less you know the better, my dear," he said rather nervously.

"Now I am worried," she said as the rain continued to pour down heavily.

"Don't be," he said in a calm tone of voice. "Are you hungry?"

"Famished!" she admitted.

"Then let's eat," he said and took out some sandwiches and fruit from his bag.

"I've brought a few things along, too," she said, and started to lay them out on the bench. There was homemade bread, lard, meat, gherkins and two slices of blueberry tart. She even had a small bottle of schnapps.

"I don't know how you Czechs stay so slim. And you've even thought of the slivovice!" Colin said impressed.

"My father made it from our own plums, but let's save that for last," she suggested.

Despite the rain they enjoyed their little outing. The cold breeze only made them huddle closer together. Colin wanted to kiss Irma, but she turned away.

"Colin. I don't know if I'm being fair to you. I had felt so confined in my sheltered little world, and then you appear to stir up my repressed desires. But what if it's just the novelty of the situation that's making us act this way? We should be reasonable, before we are both misled by our emotions." No matter what Irma said, however, her body was talking another language while she felt the butterflies flitting around in her stomach, imploring her to be near him.

"Look, we really should be heading back," Colin said in an effort to be sensible. "I don't think there's any danger of being seen together in this weather, so I'll accompany you to the bus station again, and then we'll part ways," he said and took out an envelope from his jacket. "Here's some money for the next few bus fares, and a little extra," he said as he handed it to her.

"I couldn't take any more money from you," she said, averting her eyes. "Not now, anyway."

"See it as a present from Her Majesty."

"Alright then," she agreed. She took the envelope, and balanced it with her fingertips. Then she turned to face Colin, looking longingly into his eyes. He tried to resist but something in the way she looked at him compelled him to lean over and kiss her again. They didn't stop even as the raindrops began to stream through the thick leaves of the tree and onto their faces. Eventually, Colin opened the umbrella and they continued their fervent kissing until a dog barking in the distance broke the spell they were under.

"Come now," Irma whispered as she broke away from Colin's embrace, "a bit of cold rain will bring you back down to earth," she said. She took hold of the umbrella and started to make her way briskly through the drenched grass. She smiled cheekily back at him.

"Hey wait!" he called after her. He gathered his things and caught up with Irma by the winding path.

They hardly exchanged a word on the way towards the bus station. Irma somehow feared that Colin may no longer want to see her now that she had more or less disclosed all she knew.

"I'll meet you again at the school in two days' time. Can you make it?" Colin asked intently.

"I'll be there," she nodded and looked downwards.

"Good, then let's say around six in the evening. Oh, and bring me a small photo of yourself. I want to think about you on my long trip," he finally said.

Thirty-four

Sarah couldn't help but wonder whether Thaunton had returned to collect the remaining essays before he finally waved the semester goodbye. Okay, he still had to correct and grade all those papers before he went abroad, she realised, but it would be better to check, and precisely that will give me an excuse to contact him.

> From: sarahhafner@arts-stud.melbuni.com.au
> Sent: Saturday, 31.10.2015, 14:14
> To: Mr Thaunton
> Re: semester paper
>
> Dear Mr Thaunton,
>
> Sorry to have missed you last week. I had another class that unfortunately went overtime, and it wasn't until shortly before five that I realised this. When I finally got to your office, though, the only people I saw there were several other students who were also keen to hand in their papers. We somehow managed to slot them all into your pigeonhole and then decided to celebrate the end of the semester at the Prince Alfred Hotel.
>
> I suppose you're going to be busy with corrections now, but nevertheless I hope there'll still be a chance

to meet up before you leave us for faraway shores. I currently have most of my paintings on display at the café where I work in Carlton if you'd like to see them. We have the best apple strudel in town if you like that sort of thing with your coffee. We have to lure the customers in somehow! Anyway, let me know however you decide.

Kind regards,
Sarah Hafner

From: thaunton@arts-fac.melbuni.com.au
Sent: Sunday, 01.11.2015, 16:41
To: Sarah Hafner
Re: semester paper

Dear Sarah,

I'm usually in my office until six, and I would have loved to stay and chat with you for a while, but I had to dash off to the post office before it closed to post my proposal for another conference I hope to be attending in Germany in February. Alas, fate was against us this time. But not to worry. I did notice that a few papers were missing, so I'll collect them sometime during the week. We could meet for a coffee after I've picked up the remaining papers if you like. I'm quite flexible, so just name a time and place and I'll be there. Looking forward to seeing your paintings, too.

Yours,
Thaunton

From: sarahhafner@arts-stud.melbuni.com.au
Sent: Sunday, 01.11.2015, 21:08
To: Mr Thaunton
Re: semester paper

I'll come and pick you up from your office around 6pm on Tuesday after my shift, and we can walk over. And leave some room for the strudel!

Till then!
Sarah

Thirty-five

One of the apples toppled from Irma's basket to the ground with a muted thud. It disappeared amongst all the tall blades of grass. Irma was about to turn around and look for it when her grandmother Ludmila, who was a few steps behind her, said: "Leave that one to mother nature dear. We already have enough apples here for three cakes!"

As they made their way back to her grandmother's country house, the wind buffeted at their bodies, parting Irma's hair and then blowing it in all directions. It gave her a mystical, almost surreal appearance.

Curiosity was getting the better of Ludmila: "Now tell me more about this gentleman you've met," she said while they both took off their coats and settled into the kitchen.

"His name's Colin Wood," Irma began as she washed and peeled the apples. "And he teaches English at the British Council in Brno," Irma went on, careful not to reveal too much.

"But I imagine he isn't planning on staying here indefinitely, is he?"

"Well, even if he wanted to, he couldn't, since all the teachers there are on limited contracts, normally lasting two to four years at the most," Irma said as she grated one apple after another.

"From what your mother says, you've been spending quite some time together. Does that mean we'll soon be hearing wedding bells by any chance?" Ludmila casually remarked without looking up, while her hands dexterously kneaded the dough that she would soon be rolling out in wafer-thin layers.

"Anything's possible, dear Ludmila, and to tell you the truth, I probably wouldn't refuse if he proposed to me," Irma replied. "Although, there's still so much we don't know about each other."

"Irma, take my advice," Ludmila began, and looked her granddaughter in the eyes. "Don't let this chance slip by; it may be your only way out of this country for a long time. And even if he did stay the full four years, in all likelihood things aren't going to change for the better that quickly," she stated as she pounded more dough on the kitchen bench with a strength that surprised Irma.

"You could be right there."

"You'll probably be my age before we see any democracy here again. Mark my words. And what kind of future would you have here anyway? Believe me, there's nothing I would hate more than to never be able to see one of my grandchildren again, but you must think of yourself now," she concluded, wiping the tears that began to stream down her eyes.

"Don't cry, Ludmila. We still don't know what fate has in store for us all," Irma said, and went to hug her. Since Ludmila's hands were full of flour, she was careful not to touch Irma's back. Irma observed her wrinkled and anxious face. One day, she mused, I myself will turn old and grey, and devote my time to baking cakes, knitting and looking after the grandchildren. But it could well be in England and not in familiar surroundings. What a thought! Perhaps I won't even have grandchildren. But if I did, I would teach them how to paint as soon as they were old enough. It's something I've always wanted to do, but never had the chance. Then at least, if they were any good, they would have something to leave behind once their time was up. I think it's sad that my future children won't be able to meet their great-grandmother or even their grandparents, seeing they probably won't let them out of the country once I emigrate.

"How silly that life is so short, without sufficient time to complete everything we'd like to," Ludmila finally said.

"Well," Irma began, "some artists did manage to leave behind enough paintings to fill several galleries before they died. Think of Van Gogh, for example. He was such a prolific painter, especially in the last years of his life."

"That's all well and good for some people," Ludmila said, "who have the good fortune to be able to devote their time to their hobbies. Such people probably never had to work on a farm."

"You've got a point there," agreed Irma. But then again, Irma thought to herself, he only lived to be thirty-seven. This reminded her of Jane Austen and Katherine Mansfield. Although they died young, they left behind any number of novels and short stories. What bliss it would be to lead such a carefree life devoid of normal responsibility, to be able to elevate the senses to another dimension, even if that life was relatively short. Of course, it would still be nice to live long enough to become a grandmother!

I'll tell them one day, but now definitely isn't the right time, Irma said to herself. Hopefully soon after I've safely escaped from this country, they'll find my diary, and discover what I really went through. Maybe then they'll understand why I couldn't confide in them earlier. It would have needlessly put their lives at risk as well as mine. We come from a long line of worriers, so once I was released from prison, I only briefly told my family about my friendship with Blanka, sparing them all the details of her colourful life. But little did they know at the time (nor I myself for that matter) that I was going to become involved with a spy of my own.

Thirty-six

"So from now on, you can call me *Eric*," he insisted. "As a teacher you get sick of people calling you by your surname," he explained to a wide-eyed Sarah.

"Well Mr Th...um, I mean, Eric, I'm so glad you found the time to come and see my paintings."

"So am I, Sarah," he began. "Actually I should be attending a departmental meeting that I had forgotten all about, but I just couldn't bring myself to postpone our date. So mum's the word!"

"I won't tell a soul," she promised as she raised her cup and breathed in its aroma.

"And I can see from your paintings that you've been blessed with a generous dose of talent. I should be talking about your work in my lessons," Eric said in admiration. "You'll be my guest artist next year," he persisted.

"I don't think my artistic efforts are worthy of such praise, but it's what I enjoy doing most in life." Sarah started to worry that her paintings had transfixed him more than she herself had.

"No, I'm serious," Eric began as he sipped at his cappuccino. "I find that if you look beyond the aesthetic surface, there's a kind of underlying ambiguity; something that's strikingly enticing at first glance and then irrationally elusive, if you see what I'm getting at."

"It's probably the eclectic goulash of styles I use that frustrates interpretation. But who am I to know what lurks inside me?" she said airily, wanting to see Eric laugh. He did smile, but he also wanted to get to the bottom of his analysis. Sarah, on the other hand, was keen to change tack.

"For instance, your painting entitled *best-kept secret* has an extraordinary way of seducing the beholder. Once it has your undivided attention; it makes you totally forget the world around you. Then, while you're blissfully being absorbed by it, it suddenly dawns upon you that you're trapped, not knowing where to go from there," he went on as his thoughts were being fuelled by another dose of caffeine. "And yet, instead of leaving it at that, and turning away, you find yourself desperately longing to understand something that is beyond interpretation," he concluded, looking at Sarah and expecting her to explain further. All the while, though, after having taken a deep breath, Sarah was now sighing pleasurably, seeing Eric's description of her painting as an analogy to whatever it was between them. She picked up her cup and finished the rest of her coffee before it got cold.

"Perhaps that's why it's a part of the whole series I entitled 'unexplained enigmas that are best kept secret'. Once I understand it all myself, I promise you'll be the first to know."

"I'll look forward to that," Eric began, staring deeply into her eyes. "Still, it's marvellous that people like yourself can become so passionate about their hobbies. It's rare these days to create something that can evoke so much attention," he said to her, yet all he could see were two large velvety pupils that flickered sensuously in an alluring sea of cerulean blue, irresistibly framed by her tantalising eyelashes.

"Nevertheless, I don't think my paintings are so wrapped in mystery. Perhaps it's a reflection of my neurotic way of seeing things, but I doubt whether there's more to me than meets the eye," Sarah said humbly, deciding she would not avert her eyes from Eric's for as long as she could. "It's nice to be led astray every now and then, isn't it?" Sarah said unexpectedly, which made Eric forget all about her painting.

"Maybe that's why others help us derail on purpose, so that we don't forsake life's other little joys," Eric finally replied.

For a split second Sarah lowered her eyes to place her empty cup on the saucer. As soon as she let go of it, Eric gently took her hands, and they gazed at each other until a waitress approached to ask if they wanted to order anything else. They withdrew their hands, and sensing that enough seeds of insinuation had been planted, Sarah asked for the bill, which she paid, much to Eric's discontent.

"Don't worry, you can shout me a beer at the next pub we come across," she suggested.

"Gladly!" Eric said as their hands intertwined once more.

As they left the café, they were welcomed by a balmy breeze. The world seemed delightful. They walked hand in hand down Elgin Street for about a block until they reached a second-hand guitar shop that caught Eric's attention.

"I've always wanted to check this place out," he said as they both looked through the large window.

"Wow, there are hundreds of them in there; it must be awfully difficult to make the right choice," she said, looking at the vast array of used guitars inside the shop. "I never knew you played the guitar." She gave Eric a questioning look.

"It's something I do when I manage to tear myself away from my daily obligations. I just love learning how to play jazz chords and scales until my fingers ache." He smiled. "Anyway, there are a lot of things we don't know about each other. My fantasy had been trying to fill in the gaps all semester," he admitted as they walked away from the shop, "wondering how you really are in private; whether you're ironic and witty or emotional and introverted…"

"I guess all kinds of thoughts find their misleading way into our minds before we really get to know someone."

"Still, the fact that we were able to connect at all is remarkable."

"That's true, but I think a lot depends on us. I've always believed that whatever we dream about or constantly keep in our thoughts has a way of manifesting itself into reality. Sooner or later, anyway, which is why I try to think as positively as I can," Sarah revealed.

"I need to be more like that," Eric said. "Then I could ward off all the doubts that seem to hinder what I'm really striving for. Perhaps that's another reason why we hadn't met earlier. Mea culpa, I'm afraid!"

"But it takes two to tango," she quipped. "You see, the trick is to try to pretend you already have what you wish for. Imagine it as a part of your life as vividly as you can, whether it be a suitable partner, a coveted career or any other aspirations you may have," she explained. "Lots of books have already been written on the subject, but it still takes a lot of mental discipline in the beginning. In any case, it seems to work," she concluded confidently.

"So I have to train my own imagination, do I?" he asked.

"Well, it helps and it's definitely worth the effort, since in the end, the picture will eventually turn out exactly as we have painted it," she explained. "Hey, I just made that up," she said cheerfully, "although, I'm not too sure if I used the correct tenses. Anyway, the future should correlate with what you had been imagining the whole time, um…if that makes any sense."

"Perfectly! I'll try to keep that in mind every time any negative thoughts start to prey on my mind," Eric said before turning his attention to Sarah. "And how about you? What kind of wishes are you planting in your mind at the moment?"

"Well, it's a bit pragmatic, but I'd like to meet someone who's going to be instrumental in helping me bring my work to a wider audience," she confessed. "It's still very vague, but I often try to imagine myself at my own exhibitions, welcoming prominent people, listening to art critics dissect my work and seeing my paintings sell for huge sums of money." She stopped, suddenly becoming lost in thought. "In any case, it's all about sowing the seeds in your mind, but…" she hesitated.

"It requires a lot of patience," he added.

"I know," she began, "I've been waiting for this all year!" She turned towards Eric, let go of his hand and flung her arms around his neck. They stood there in the middle of the street kissing for several minutes whilst the traffic whizzed past them.

"I think we're in the way," Eric realised as a stranger's arm brushed past his.

"Just one more kiss," she pleaded, "or perhaps two…"

Thirty-seven

"Three, four...five, six...seven, eight, nine," Irma counted under her breath. After making sure all of Colin's students had left the building, she decided the coast was clear. She crossed the road from the bus stop, where she had been pretending to wait for a bus. Staying there any longer might have drawn attention to herself, seeing that three buses had already passed.

Colin saw her coming up the stairs, and in the doorway they kissed for quite a while before saying anything.

"I'm so glad you're back," she whispered.

"I'm glad to be here; I missed you terribly," he said while he closed the door. "Shall we go to a pub for a bite to eat?"

"I'm not used to eating so late, but perhaps we could share something then," she suggested.

"Splendid, there's a jolly nice place down the road called 'The Grumpy Goose', where the food is as good as the beer," he proposed.

"Lead the way!"

Despite the smoke, the place was rather cosy. After indulging in a few beers and culinary specialities, Colin brought Irma back to his place. It was only a very small one-bedroom flat with a kitchen and bathroom but more than enough for Colin's purposes. The bed could be converted to a couch by day, and there was also a small desk where Colin worked.

"You really shouldn't have, Colin!" Irma objected while he placed the array of goods next to her on the couch. "Mandarines, bananas and all these chocolates! I can't possibly accept them all."

"I told you I'd bring you a few souvenirs from home," he began and sat down next to her. "Anyway, now you'll have a good excuse for your nosy neighbour as to why you came to Brno today," he said to justify his generosity.

"I'm sure she'll believe me when I tell her I had to queue for several hours for these mandarines!"

"Good, that leaves me with some more time to enjoy your company," he said teasingly.

"Mmh, what do you have in mind?" she said, giving her seducer a coy smile of invitation.

"Only to have my wicked way with you," he said, and started to kiss her on the nape of her neck. "Um…with your permission, of course," he added, before noticing that she had already unbuttoned her blouse.

Thirty-eight

"I've always loved the way you look," Eric said, absorbing Sarah's beauty with his eyes and mentally shutting out the other guests at the pub they had chanced upon. "Of course, I never let on, as I felt that someone might eventually notice something," he said in reflection. "Sometimes I have the feeling that my face and body give me away, no matter what I'm thinking."

"I don't think anything about your behaviour was obvious to anyone except Dorothy."

"Did she say anything?" he enquired.

"She alluded to it a few times, but I did my best to be as uncooperative as possible. Still, I have the impression that she has some kind of uncanny access to other people's feelings," Sarah explained. "She's very perceptive in that regard, but you needn't worry about her."

"Well, it's just that…" Eric said in a slightly awkward way, "it may sound silly…um, but relationships at university can be rather tricky."

"I suppose you're right, although the term is over…" Sarah began. "I really hadn't given it much thought. I guess my head is more in my paintings…" she concluded.

After an unusually long silence, Eric took hold of her hand.

"Look, Eric," Sarah said with a sudden look of dismay.

"In two weeks' time I won't even be able to see you, let alone get to know you the way I'd like to," she continued, "and although it's deliciously tempting, the thought of throwing ourselves head over heels into a romance that will be on hold for several months unsettles me."

"You could always come along…" he said cheerfully.

"Not at such short notice, I couldn't. There's my job, preparations for another exhibition and other obligations I have to my grandparents, for example," she objected. "Don't get me wrong, I'd really love to. But then it mightn't be fair on you, since you'll be busy teaching, giving papers and generally putting more feathers in your cap. I'd only be in your way."

"I'm sure we could organise something, but most flights would probably be booked out by now."

"Alas, destiny appears to be against us once again."

"I'll send you postcards," Eric promised.

"I'll expect one from every city you visit," she said, before Eric leaned over and kissed her again, trying to defy the sobering effect of their conversation.

"Don't worry, Eric," Sarah began. "Whatever is meant to be, will be in the end. At the right time and place."

"And if not, then we're going to have to start imagining how we'd like our reciprocal destinies to unfold."

"You can't freeze love, you know," she retorted. "Let's just live our lives, come what may."

Thirty-nine

"You're safe here, well...for the time being anyway," Colin added, not without some consternation as they lay in his bed in the dark.

"I still haven't got used to this world of adventure that you've lured me into," Irma said, staring at the ceiling with its intricate patterns.

"Have I? Oh, no," he shook his head. "Someone else is responsible for that; those seeds had long been sown by Blanka, remember?"

"I suppose you're right," she admitted.

"If you'd never met her, you wouldn't be caught up in all this turmoil now," he pointed out.

"That's true, but then I would never have met you, and we wouldn't be enjoying this wonderful whirlwind romance!" she said, snuggling up to him.

"Perhaps it'll last a little longer than you think," Colin whispered and started to kiss her again.

"Stop it, we've both been exceedingly naughty this evening. Possibly even enough to get me into trouble. Anyway," she went on, "once you return to your royal island, I'll be left here all by myself."

"No you won't, since I'm taking you with me!" he said resolutely.

*

Irma awoke to find herself alone in Colin's bed. In her dreamy languor she looked curiously about his flat. Somehow it had looked different last night, she thought. To the left of the bed there was a large window covered by thin curtains with a cream and faded-brown floral design. There was also a large pot plant, a cupboard in one corner, a chair and a desk with many books piled on top of it. Next to the bed she noticed a large clock ticking away and was astonished that it hadn't kept her awake all night. I wonder where he's gone; perhaps he's just popped out to buy some breakfast, she speculated, and slowly got up. Irma opened the window, and the familiar smell of cabbage pervaded the air. I'll miss that smell when I'm in England, she mused. Wait a minute, whatever am I going on about? It was only a dream, nothing but wishful thinking. I'd be too homesick anyway. She closed the window and headed towards the bathroom.

After Irma had freshened up, Colin opened the door, holding a paper bag full of various pastries. Some had nut fillings and others a sweet poppy-seed mixture he knew she liked.

"Ah, Sleeping Beauty has awoken," he said as they approached each other and kissed intensely. Irma suddenly lowered her head and bit off the end of one of the pastries which protruded from the bag. "Eww," she disapproved, "that one's for you. Nut-filling!"

"I'll go and prepare some tea," he said as he went into the kitchen. Meanwhile Irma sat down on the edge of the bed and ate heartily. She then gave the huge plant some much-needed water.

"What do you have in store for us today?" she asked as Colin entered the bedroom with a pot of tea and two cups.

"I'm afraid our days in Brno are numbered, darling Irma," he announced suddenly.

"But you've only just come back; don't tell me you're

leaving me already!" A look of anguish appeared on her face. "Not just yet," she pleaded.

"As a matter of fact, you're going to have to put up with me a little longer, for I have received strict orders to take you with me," he answered as he poured some tea into both cups.

"I don't understand."

"Look Irma, I've known this all along, but I didn't know when would be a good time to tell you," he began and then fell silent.

"Please explain, Colin."

"You're coming to the UK with me," he went on.

"But why? I've already told you everything I know. Are your superiors going to try to torture more information out of me?" she asked cynically.

"No, nothing like that, believe me Irma," he took her in his arms. "I would never let anyone harm you," he said reassuringly. "It's just that, well, you know too much, and they fear that you may eventually speak to the wrong people. That's all."

"I'm not at all like Blanka, you know. I wouldn't even know who to approach," she persisted.

"I know, but that's not the problem. You see, they know how to approach you, and in all likelihood they soon will. So you can't blame our lot for not wanting to take any chances. They're desperate to keep the information about the mole under wraps, as well as all the other things you reported to me," he said and sipped his tea calmly.

"Will I be in any danger?"

"Not at all. I'll be there to help you, so you needn't worry."

"And if I refuse to come with you?"

"Then I'm to kill you," he said airily.

"What!"

"Oh, come now, I'd sooner die myself than have you harmed in any way."

"Have you ever killed anyone?"

"No, I let the others do all the dirty work," he admitted pragmatically.

"This is really all too sudden. Anyway, how on earth do you plan to get me out of this well-guarded country? I don't even have a passport, and even if I did, they would send me back before you could bat an eyelid. Every border crossing is patrolled. There's no way we could possibly leave the country officially or even illegally, for that matter."

"Oh, yes there is," Colin reassured her. He let go of her and walked over to the opened cupboard near the window. He reached for something inside one of his coats, and then handed her a British passport.

"Why are you showing me your passport?" she asked.

"It's not mine," he said nonchalantly. He couldn't wait to see her face when she opened the document.

"Oh my God, it's me! And you've used the photo I gave you. Now I know why you wanted my picture so badly. But however did you manage to forge it?"

"Anything is possible with connections in high places," he explained. "The Foreign Office always cooperates with us."

"There's another name on it. Who is this woman?"

"Um…that's my wife," he said offhandedly. Irma was struck speechless and went very pale.

"So you are married after all," she finally said in a state of mild shock. "And what does she think of all this?"

"Nothing at all. You see, to her, I'm just a teacher working abroad."

"So you're an unfaithful liar!"

"Well, apart from the fact that my job strictly forbids me to disclose certain information, I wouldn't want to burden my wife with such realities. As for being unfaithful, well, my emotions seem to have clearly won the tug of war against good sense and morality." Colin's voice suddenly filled with urgency. "Yet the main thing now is to get us both out of this country, so we'll have to postpone matters of the heart until that is accomplished."

"But even if we manage to get out of Czechoslovakia, won't the British authorities assume you're trying to smuggle me in illegally?" she asked, trying to think logically.

"That's why my wife and son were sent to Australia for an indefinite period, to make an identity available for you. Of course, she thinks it's the Council just shuffling me around the globe, but better that than have her worry herself to death."

"And you have a child as well."

"I'm afraid so."

She lowered her eyes and stared at the passport. "My, my, they really think of everything, don't they?" She shook her head. "All this trouble just to get me out of the country, papers and all!"

"Of course, it's only temporary. You'll receive your own papers once we make you a British citizen. Just see it as your only way to freedom," he said as he poured himself another cup of tea.

"And what did you tell your wife?" Irma wanted to know. "I imagine you'll be joining her in Australia as soon as you've delivered me to your superiors."

"Well, the information you gave us about Soviet and Czech spies operating in Australia turned out to be true, so it won't be long before I'm sent there to help the secret service save the country from the clutches of communism. Officially, though, I'll have a government job, teaching English to new immigrants. Yet I'll do everything I can to stay with you for as long as possible."

"But even if all goes well, you'll be leaving me in the end," she said as the tears welled up in her eyes.

Forty

My period is five days late, thought Lucinda as she brushed her teeth; I've never had such a long cycle before. I definitely can't have been ovulating the last time we… No, there's nothing to worry about; I've had late periods before, and besides he did pull out just in time. I'm sure of that since my whole belly was covered with his semen; a puddle of it formed around my belly button, and some of it even reached my face and got stuck in several strands of hair. To stop the rest of it dripping onto the sheets, I smeared it into the pores of my skin. I guess there could be the remotest chance that a minute sample re-entered me, either then or as I was showering it off my body afterwards. I wonder how many women have actually become pregnant that way.

Lucinda spat out the water and frothy tooth paste before looking in the mirror to see if everything was okay. Karel entered the bathroom, his hair standing up in all directions.

"Hey, I love your morning look," Lucinda began. "You should simply gel it so that it stays that way all day," she suggested.

"You can't imagine how oily my hair actually is. Even if I did use gel, it probably wouldn't be long before it returned to its lifeless state," he explained.

"Anyway, good morning! How did you sleep?" Lucinda enquired.

"Terribly," he grumbled. "After you had read out so much of your grandmother's diary yesterday evening, I couldn't think of anything else and even dreamed about her! And how was your night?"

"Good, but I've been feeling a bit funny the last few days. I think I may be pregnant." The words took Karel by surprise.

"Really? But we've been so careful. I mean anything's possible, seeing that you're not on the pill and you can't stand condoms. But isn't your period meant to be around about now?"

"Precisely, but it is several days late," she explained. "Oh, I'll just wait another day or two before I start jumping to conclusions," she said resolutely.

"But then again, I guess I'm old enough to be a father," Karel concluded.

"Well, don't count your chickens before they're hatched!"

Forty-one

Having both passed her exams and over three months' holidays to look forward to, Sarah had every reason to be cheerful, but she was sad. Eric had already flown off to Europe, so she felt she had to immerse herself in her painting, especially now that she had so much time on her hands. Anyway, time would fly as it always does, and Eric would be back by the beginning of next semester. But anything could happen during his stay in the Old World. He'll probably meet the woman of his dreams, move to Europe and forget all about me, she dramatised. If only we had met earlier, she sighed as she cleared away the cups from a table where the last guests for that day had been sitting not long ago.

Sarah was just about to close up for the evening when that nice young man who had been eager to buy one of her paintings a few months ago suddenly appeared.

"I'm afraid we're closed for the day," Sarah said, placing one of the chairs on top of a table.

"I don't know if you remember me, but I just wanted to pick up one of your paintings," he said almost apologetically.

"Oh, hello!" Sarah said brightly upon recognising the man. "Of course, please take a seat," she said as she made her way to the front door and locked it behind her. "Would you like anything to drink? I can make you a tea, coffee or a hot chocolate?"

"A hot chocolate would be fine, but only if it's not too much trouble," he said.

"Coming right up," she said and darted behind the counter.

Sarah reminded him of a dragonfly as he watched her moving swiftly from one end of the café to another. He sat on a stool behind the counter and enjoyed observing her erratic movements.

"But please, take your time; I'm in no hurry," he said. "I'm Alan by the way."

"Pleased to make your acquaintance," she said in a louder voice, for the milk-frothing machine resonated throughout the whole place. "I'm Sarah."

"I just love English accents; you all sound so well-spoken," he said frankly.

"I have been doing my best to australianize the way I talk."

"Oh, don't ever change it, please," he said almost beseechingly.

"I was born and bred in England, although my grandfather has some Czech and German roots," she said.

"My ancestors have been here a bit longer, but it probably wasn't interesting enough for my relatives to want to find out more about their past, which is a shame."

"Perhaps you should start to delve into your family tree," she suggested as she placed the two drinks in front of them and took a seat next to him. "Here's the sugar in case it's too bitter for you; I always find it disgustingly sweet unless I make it myself."

"No, I prefer it that way too," he said after taking a sip. "Mmh, it's exquisite!"

They chatted for the best part of an hour, and although Sarah found that they didn't have that much in common, she liked the man nevertheless, especially his physical appearance, and promised to let him know when she would be organising another exhibition.

Forty-two

Like so many times before, it turned out to be a false alarm. Lucinda's period had arrived. She was bleeding more than usual this time round and on days like these she liked to laze around the flat. To distract herself, she decided to read the last few pages of the diary Milena had given her. She soon reached a page where Irma had been preoccupied with similar woes…

Really it's the last thing I need now. As if things weren't already bad enough! And to find out that he's married with a son and has been using a false name all along. Still, I'm not going to trouble him with my anxiety. Lord knows he has enough on his mind at the moment. If only I had kept my trap shut a year ago; a lot of good lashing out at someone does you! I would neither have gone to prison nor met Blanka, and above all I wouldn't be in this predicament right now! I wonder what else fate has in store for me? Here I am lying in my own bed, possibly for the last time, and I'm not allowed to tell anyone about it until we're safely out of the country. That's so unfair. But I'm sure my family will understand. Once I'm in England, I'll inform them all. Yet how? Any letters are bound to be censored and I dread the thought of them eventually finding out from the authorities that I've emigrated. No matter what the scoundrels say, there's not going to be a scintilla of truth in it, knowing them. I'll just have to write my sister a letter and have it delivered by another spy. In the meantime, my family will be worried senseless, so I must leave a note in a place where someone will find it after we've crossed the border. I wonder what life's going to be like in Britain…

Forty-three

Sarah still couldn't believe her luck. It was a bright Monday morning, and she had just spent the weekend in Bendigo. She hadn't really been thrilled about going such a long way to celebrate an old friend's birthday, but now she was glad she had made the effort. Her best friend from her teaching days had already chosen one of her paintings as a present, so it would have been awkward to cancel anyway. In the end she'd had a lovely time, but more importantly, by a strange twist of fate, she had met an influential person from the art world who saw something special in her painting. She needed to tell someone all about it, for she was quite hopeless at keeping things to herself. She immediately decided to ring Dorothy, to whom she had already confided her little rendezvous with Eric. Dorothy was still in her pyjamas and didn't particularly feel like leaving the flat that day, so she invited Sarah around to her place for breakfast on condition that she brought along a large Capricciosa pizza with her.

"Mmh!" Dorothy visibly relished her unconventional breakfast.

"You're the only person I know who can get terribly excited about eating pizza so early in the day."

"I can eat it any time, but now I need my coffee," she said as her Bialetti moka pot started to gurgle loudly on the stovetop. She took out two small cups and poured them both some coffee. "I'll just see if I have any milk left," she said, and took out a carton from the fridge. She poured its contents into a small pot and began to attack it vigorously with her milk frother.

"While you're going to all this trouble, do you have any cocoa powder I could sprinkle on the foam?" asked Sarah.

"I have a much better alternative!" She took out a piece of dark chocolate from the pantry, and grated it directly into Sarah's cup.

"Mmh, lovely! Thank you, my dear."

"Now what is it that you're so eager to tell me about?" she asked as she ravenously gorged on another slice of pizza.

"Well, I don't know where to begin. Um..." She thought for a while. "We've always wanted to work as professional painters, haven't we?" she began. "Yet what chance do we actually have of being discovered these days?"

"Hmm," Dorothy pondered, chewing another mouthful enthusiastically. "The selection process can be somewhat crude, reserved for a fortunate few who are able to impress the right people," she said cynically. "Both of us are currently selling our paintings for a pittance..."

"That is, if we manage to sell them in the first place," Sarah added.

"Still, I think we're entitled to a little more recognition," Dorothy went on. "You probably just need to get your first break, that's all."

"Precisely," agreed Sarah. "Well, guess what? During my weekend away I happened to meet a very prominent gentleman who appreciated one of my paintings, which..." she hesitated, "mightn't mean much in the end, but..." Sarah stopped as if unsure how to continue, for her thoughts were all topsy-turvy.

"So how did you meet this guy?" Dorothy persisted, taking her cup in both hands.

"Oh, it was thanks to my absolutely atrocious sense of direction, believe it or not," Sarah confessed. "I had been invited to a birthday party in Bendigo by Rachel, a former colleague of mine."

"What made her move up there?"

"While we were both still teachers, she got married to a wealthy wine maker and she soon moved to his winery. It's not far from the town, but it must be somewhat isolated. Well, anyway, she had invited us all to this posh restaurant, which was just off one of the main roads near the historical tramline. 'It used to be a bank in the nineteenth century,' she said. 'You can't miss it!' she insisted," Sarah imitated her friend's instructions whilst raising her eyebrows.

Dorothy smiled. "Yet you failed to notice any restaurant that apparently couldn't be missed…"

"Exactly!" Sarah confirmed, taking another sip of her coffee. "It wasn't surprising, as practically all the buildings in the old town used to be banks, what with the gold rush and all."

"There also must have been quite a few brothels, I imagine," Dorothy interrupted her.

"True, um…so there I was with this huge painting under my arm – it was Rachel's birthday present by the way. You remember, the still life with a nude by the window staring at a flower in a vase."

"I know the one," Dorothy recalled.

"Anyway, I was at a loss where to go first. So after having crossed the tram tracks, I started to make my way up the street, for she told me it was near an army disposals shop, which I easily spotted."

"But still no sign of an ex-bank?" enquired Dorothy playfully.

"Hang on, it's coming!" Sarah tried to explain. "Not really knowing where to go…"

"Why didn't you just ask a passer-by?"

"I guess it's the masculine side to my DNA that prevents me from asking complete strangers for directions. So I ventured up the road, simply following my intuition, as it was such a charming street full of lovely little antique shops and cafés."

"It can't have been easy, you being laden with that enormous painting, but do go on."

"I eventually chanced upon a building that resembled more a court of justice than a bank, for it had these thick columns alongside the entrance. But I decided to go in anyway, as there were people standing outside drinking wine and chatting amiably. Not the sort of crowd Rachel would associate with, so I just supposed they were her husband's acquaintances. After I had bravely entered the imposing building, I furtively passed through a long hallway that had little rooms on either side before it turned into a charming little wine bar with cosy tables and a fireplace. And there were wine bottles stacked right up to the ceiling."

"Yet still no sign of the birthday girl and her entourage?"

"Unfortunately not. I was desperately trying to spot a familiar face, but before I could continue to scan the interior, I found myself amongst a besuited crowd, who were staring and gesturing at a series of paintings on the walls."

"As good as that, were they?"

"Well the majority of guests certainly seemed to be overwhelmed by them, but I thought they were downright grotesque! I couldn't believe my eyes. And then I realised to my embarrassment that I must have been at a vernissage rather than an innocent social gathering, seeing that there were elegant women all trying to upstage one another and black-clad pseuds going on about some up-and-coming artist while flicking strands of hair out of their eyes. The whole place was crackling with chin-stroking arrogance."

"Well, I'm sure some people feel at home in that kind of environment," Dorothy began ironically. "Anyhow, I imagine you left there quick smart."

"I would have liked to, but the place was teeming with people, and it was becoming rather difficult to move with Rachel's present clutched under my arm. Then some self-important galah, who wasn't looking where he was going, spilled some of his wine only centimetres away from my painting when he ran into me."

"Oh dear!"

"Then after giving me a brief apologetic smile, he suddenly bellowed out to someone he recognised across the room: 'Oh Gavin, there you are! I simply must have a word with you.' So seeing a suitable gap, I made a dash for the doorway, through which a waiter appeared and tried to thrust a glass of wine in my direction. I shook my head, managed to squeeze through to the front room and headed towards the main entrance. A woman who had just arrived actually thought I had bought one of the horrid exhibits! 'Oh, good,' she said, 'looks like they're going to sell like hot cakes today,' and then just as I was about to…"

"It's a wonder no one thought you were stealing it," interrupted Dorothy.

"Strangely enough, I did feel like I was up to something devious. Anyway, as I was making my way out of there, I took one last surreptitious look back, and then it happened…"

"You damaged the painting!"

"Luckily not. But in my haste I accidentally bumped into

a man wearing a tweed jacket and made him drop his plate of cheese. I immediately apologised, put down my painting, and helped him pick up the broken pieces of his plate. We were still on our knees when he suddenly spotted my painting. You'd never believe it, but he couldn't take his eyes off it! I later discovered he was some sort of agent working for an influential art dealer."

"So serendipitous encounters really do exist," Dorothy said as she started to make herself some more coffee.

"And not only did he help me find Rachel's restaurant in the end, he also wants to see all I've ever painted," Sarah said excitedly.

"You lucky girl! You never know, he may turn out to pave the way for a new career."

"That would be nice, wouldn't it! I'll tell him all about you as well," Sarah promised.

"Please do. Anyway, how many courses did you miss?"

"They had just ordered their main meals, but I was too excited to think about food. I can't even remember what I ordered, come to think of it. Dessert was pecan ice-cream in a sea of cognac, which at least brought me back down to earth."

"Were you still counting your blessings?" Dorothy asked as her moka pot started to rumble and sputter.

"Well, it was like entering another dimension and then coming back to reality. In any case, I'll never forget that fateful encounter…"

Forty-four

"That looks nice," the man said. "But it's not part of today's collection. Mind if I take a closer look?" Silence accompanied his scouring eyes. "Did you paint it?"

"Yes, it's actually a present for a friend of mine. If I ever find her, that is. You see, I seem to have erred into the wrong venue. I'm not really meant to be here at all," Sarah admitted somewhat guiltily.

"It's marvellous," he began, whilst lifting it upon a case of wine bottles to have a better look at it. "It's like a breath of fresh air compared to today's dreary collection!" he stated bluntly.

"Well, I'm sure anything would look good alongside those eyesores!" Sarah smiled, relieved she wasn't the only one who disapproved of the oeuvres on display. "Anyway, I'm glad you like my painting, but I'm afraid it's taken," she said candidly.

All the while people and waiters were passing the two. A waiter knelt down to offer them some wine: "A local Merlot from 2009. It shows deep layered aromas of blueberry, plum, chocolate with a tinge of tomato."

Sarah couldn't resist this time and found herself sniffing profusely for a tomato scent.

"He's right, you know," she ascertained, brimming with delight.

"Cheers!" they said, echoing each other.

"It's delicious!" Sarah said after taking a gulp.

"Mmh! I think I also detect a touch of vanilla. Reminds me of a superb 1996 Coonawarra I once tried," he reflected before changing the subject. "Well, I'm glad you lost your way; otherwise, who knows, I probably would never have got to see this gem of yours. Do you have any more like this one?" he asked while he relished another sip.

"Well it was part of a series of paintings entitled *Lucinda's Secrets* that were all recently hanging in a small café in Carlton."

"I must take a look at them. And if they're anything as good as this one, then we could have them exhibited where more influential people could see them," Sarah's new admirer suggested optimistically. "Oh sorry, my name's Paolo Procházka."

"Sarah Hafner. Pleased to meet you. Hey isn't *Paolo* an Italian name?"

"My mother's Italian. Father's Czech. Quite a lively combination!"

"I had a childhood friend who had a Czech grandmother. We grew up together in England. I've also been working on a nostalgic series of paintings about that part of my life."

"Good, I see you're quite a prolific painter. I would like to see every one of them. Here's my card. We should meet up sometime next week to discuss your work."

"I'd very much like that."

"And I wouldn't mind another glass of this wine! Hey, why don't you just buy your friend a case of this magical Merlot and keep this painting for a future exhibition?" suggested Paolo.

"Oh, I couldn't do that. Her husband's a wine grower himself."

"No, that wouldn't do at all," he conceded.

"And besides, she was a close friend at university and we both ended up teaching at the same school, so I gave her first pick from all the paintings that didn't sell, yet I'm sure she could lend it to me if need be."

"What did you study?"

"Well, I did my Bachelor of Science many years ago, followed by a brief teaching career, and now I'm back at university, in the process of finishing an Arts degree," Sarah explained.

"And are you reaping the harvest of your new academic life?"

"To a certain extent. It allows me to paint more, and I do a bit of waitressing on the side so that I can exhibit my paintings in cafés."

"Oh, sorry to interrupt you, Sarah, but there's an art critic here whom I particularly dislike," he said whilst leading Sarah into the main part of the gallery. All the while she tried to keep an eye on her abandoned painting.

"Precociously talented!" praised a man in a bright orange shirt.

"Hm," said the man who had bumped into Sarah earlier.

"Obscure, yet sufficiently delineated, I think."

"Yes, indeed, I'll have to agree with you there and I admit it's quite captivating the way she seems to have depicted the Australian bush at dusk, but…"

"What?"

"Can't you see? The twilight scene somehow seems to be confined in the branches of the banksia tree. The light should be pervading the whole scenery. Here it appears too trapped for my liking."

"Oh yes, I see what you mean. She's deliberately trying to subdue this otherwise harsh landscape."

"Exactly! Very unlike her last series of paintings that were so realistic in comparison."

"I suppose her mind is simply unfettered by the laws of nature!"

Sarah wanted to listen to more, but Paolo's eyebrows signalled her to move on. He pretended to be interested in another painting towards one corner of the room where several people, including one of today's featured artists, were in the middle of an animated exchange.

"First comes a hiatus; then by the sheer force of an unexpected catalyst I find myself being jolted into the whole process of painting. Once I start on a certain theme, I tend to relax and it can be quite therapeutic. I used to paint constantly; it was a kind of self-medication."

"The comments people make about my paintings inevitably help me think more deeply about the colours I normally use. I'm still wondering whether I had used a trifle too much cornflower blue in this painting, for example."

"The absurdity or sheer pointlessness of life is a recurring theme in his paintings."

"I disagree. We know this was untrue, mainly because of what the painter himself has since written in various publications on his own works."

"Well, up to a certain extent the good critics sometimes help put things into perspective, which can also be quite frustrating when I suddenly realise that I don't understand my work at all."

"It'll probably get much worse," Pablo warned, "so perhaps you should finally join your friends." They both made their way towards the exit. Sarah was relieved to find her painting unscathed, and carefully picked it up.

"Yes, I really must be going," Sarah agreed. "I'm so late I wouldn't be surprised if they had already sent out a search party."

"And do call me next week."

"Will do," she nodded eagerly. "Lovely meeting you!"

"Likewise. I'll show you the way," he said in front of the building.

"If you just point me in the right direction, I'll be fine," Sarah assured him.

Forty-five

"I wonder how they got out of the country in the end," Karel said after Lucinda had read out the last page of Irma's diary. Karel was taking photos of Lucinda's new haircut while she relaxed on the sofa.

"Hard to tell, as I don't have the sequel unfortunately," Lucinda replied, as Karel merrily clicked away. "I'd also like to know what happened during her first few years in Britain and whatever became of Colin or whatever his real name was."

"Didn't she mention anything else in her diary?" asked Karel. "And just when I was enjoying your daily updates on your grandmother's notorious past."

"I imagine he soon emigrated to Australia and left Irma to her fate. She eventually met my grandfather, a Slovakian immigrant who had managed to leave the country before things started to get really nasty back in 1948. They ended up having two children: my mother and aunt Veronika, whom I've already told you about."

"Perhaps there's another diary hidden at your great-aunt's place?"

"She told me that's all there was."

"Well at least you know most of Irma's story," he said. "With a bit of editing, Irma could have converted her diary into an autobiography or disguised it as a spy novel," Karel surmised.

"I think she had other things on her mind once she got to Britain," Lucinda explained.

"Well, perhaps later after she had settled down and digested it all." Karel speculated while Lucinda tried to smile provocatively into the camera.

"Well, you'd have to have nerves of steel to digest everything she went through."

Putting his camera down, he snuggled up to Lucinda and began to kiss her passionately.

"Your new hairstyle is giving me naughty thoughts."

"I'm bleeding like a cow, I'm afraid." She lowered her head. "But could you give me a nice massage instead? My neck and back are killing me," she complained.

"Okay, come here, and let me knead all the tension out of you," he said as he started to massage her shoulders.

"Mmmh, that feels good," she moaned. "A little higher… to the left… When you're finished," she said in a lascivious tone, "I'll spoil you in other ways…"

Forty-six

"Merry Christmas!" Emma, William and Sarah exclaimed in unison as George opened the door.

"A merry Christmas to you, too!" he echoed as he took everyone inside. "I hope you're all hungry after your journey, for lunch is just about ready."

"Sorry we're late, I spent an eternity skyping with my parents," Emma explained.

"How are they doing?"

"Oh, they're well. They decided to spend the festive season in Guernsey and see the island properly while there aren't any tourists about."

"They're quite game! It must be freezing at this time of year."

"Considering the horrible heatwave we've been having, I actually envy them," Sarah said as she started to fan her face with a Christmas card she had randomly picked up from a nearby table.

Just like every year, the two Hafner families spent Christmas Day together up in the country where it was usually not as swelteringly hot as in the outer suburbs of Melbourne. Emma was eternally grateful that every year William's mother would readily take on the laborious task of cooking roast goose, red cabbage and dumplings. And this year there was going to be the added bonus of watching the Downton Abbey Christmas special on TV. Both avid fans, Margaret and Emma never missed an episode of their favourite series. At first, William didn't quite comprehend what all the fuss was about, but after watching only three episodes he became hopelessly addicted himself. Yet before the topic of conversation would turn to the vagaries of the Downton characters, slices of Emma's Christmas stollen were devoured, coffees and whiskies savoured and presents exchanged. Apart from these rituals of indulgence, George cherished every opportunity to see the people who were dearest to him. With mixed feelings he still held onto the stylish pen that Sarah had given him.

The air had become pleasantly balmy, so they all went into the garden for a stroll. Whilst Margaret was busy showing Emma and William her rhododendrons, George took Sarah aside to a far corner of their huge garden.

"I've got a big favour to ask of you, my dear girl," he announced out of the blue.

"Anything for you, Bedřich," Sarah said with a smile.

"You know that for some time now I've been working on my autobiography, don't you?" he asked, keeping his voice down.

"Yes, I heard, and we're all looking forward to reading it."

"Well, I'll soon be needing your help to finish it, Sarah."

"My help?" She gave him a questioning look.

"It's my eyesight, you see; I'm starting to have some trouble focussing on my writing," he explained. "I'm going to have to limit how much I write each day, which is a shame, especially now that I have such a beautiful pen," he went on. "So I'd like to dictate parts of it to you. Only if you think you're up to it, of course, I mean time-wise."

"No problem. It'll be a pleasure to assist you with your intriguing project," she said eagerly.

"You're most kind. There's not that much to do really, probably a matter of just filling in bits here and there. And I still have to come up with a proper ending. Apart from that, it would be lovely if you could read some of it back to me, in case I want to change anything. But I wouldn't want to take up too much of your time, so perhaps you could come every second Wednesday afternoon, for instance. That's when Margaret has cream tea with her friends Evelyne and Gwendolyn. How does that sound?"

"Yes, let's do it like that," she agreed.

"Splendid! There's just one thing, um…" he hesitated. "Not a word to your grandmother, for there are a few chapters of my life that I've been keeping secret since I arrived in Australia."

"For so long? Wow," she went on, "I don't think I could keep anything to myself for longer than a few days!"

"No, humans are not meant to keep secrets," George said. "Actually it's quite unnatural, and even though it's stored away in the hidden depths of your mind, you can never really erase it forever."

"Perhaps writing about it is a way of getting it out of your system once and for all. It's probably just as therapeutic as painting," Sarah concluded.

"I sincerely hope so. Anyway, before you leave this evening, I'll give you the first fifty pages to take home," he suggested.

"Very well. I'll type them out on my computer and save them for you. Perhaps we'll even be able to have your book published one day!" she said excitedly.

"You're an optimistic creature, aren't you?"

"I have to be; otherwise I probably wouldn't exhibit a single painting."

"That's different. You have talent. I can't stop admiring the painting you gave me for my last birthday. It's so delightful!"

"I'm glad you like it, and you've found a nice spot for it in the house. Whatever happened to that painting that used to hang in your living room?"

"Well, after forty odd years that old thing had somehow outstayed its welcome," he recollected.

"I rather liked that painting. It had something of a timeless quality about it," she began. "Just like yourself, Bedřich!"

"Unfortunately, my time is slowly running out," he said more earnestly.

"Don't say that! You're still fit and healthy, so count your blessings!"

"You're right, one mustn't grumble. It certainly would be nice to make it past one hundred; my father was just two years short of his century, you know. Worked hard his whole life and never became sedentary. That's the secret I guess."

"Do you think a hundred years is enough to accomplish everything in life, Bedřich?"

"Well, I wouldn't say no to another hundred if it were possible, but…"

"I read somewhere that a brilliant geneticist has had a scientific breakthrough in reversing the ageing process in mice, but there's probably still some way to go until it works on humans."

"It'll be too late for us, I'm afraid, but perhaps there's hope for your generation. Imagine, then you could continue to paint and make more people happy!"

"I don't know, maybe I would do something else with my life and try to stay happy myself."

Forty-seven

Luhačovice, 28th December 2015

Dear Veronika,

Can't believe Christmas is already over. And it's actually the first time I've spent it away from home. Pity you weren't there when I skyped with mum and dad. I'm really starting to miss everyone – well it has been six months since I left you all. Karel and I spent Chrissy at his parents' place, and now we're at Klara's. She kindly invited us to her little holiday house up in Luhačovice. It's such a cute little spa town. Even without all the snow that has been falling over the past few days, the village has something of a fairy-tale character. We've been having so much fun trying all sorts of natural mineral waters from the sources (so far no adverse effects, so they must be doing us some good) and going for long walks, which is just as well, considering Klara's wicked cuisine. She keeps cooking things I can't resist!

Apart from the things I had already told you about Irma's past last time we chatted, I haven't discovered anything significantly new here at Klara's, other than a letter that was clandestinely delivered by another agent shortly after she had arrived in Britain. It describes in detail how she and her spy friend managed to flee the country. Klara let me make a photocopy, so I'll have another souvenir to show you. Yet I think I've just about exhausted Milena and Klara's knowledge, so the mystery now boils down to what happened in England and what role that spy nicknamed 'Colin' played in her new life. Neither Milena nor Klara know much about him.

There are so many things I'd like to ask Irma when I visit you at Easter. I'll even bring Karel along, if I haven't scared him off by then!

Lots of love,
Lucinda

Exeter, 1st January 2016

Dear Lucy,

My, my, you're a born sleuth, aren't you? You probably inherited it from Irma. Look dear, you've succeeded in finding out so much already. I suggest you simply mention to Irma the fact that Milena revealed a few things to you about her, but try not to press her for more information. You never know, perhaps she'll tell you of her own accord. She told me the other day that she'd like to give you some jewellery that she's got locked away in some safe.

Your Karel friend sounds worth hanging on to. Do bring him to England, so we can have a closer look at him. Being a photographer, he'll have plenty of things to take pictures of in Devon. And how's your painting coming along? Have you actually managed to find the time despite being involved in so many other activities?

Anyway whatever you do, bundle up well and keep warm during this time of year. Here all sorts of nasty viruses are confining people to their beds. I've been feeling croaky all week, so I'll have to start eating more ginger, honey and garlic.

Happy New Year!
Veronika

Forty-eight

It wasn't like Sarah to be late for an opening of an exhibition, especially when she was one of the five artists being featured, but she had simply lost track of time that afternoon. She was neither in a rush nor had she got up late. It was just that every time she had a few hours to spare, she would start doing all sorts of odd chores around the house, such as dusting or cleaning out a cupboard. Becoming preoccupied with something often distracted Sarah from more imminent obligations until a peek at the clock brought her back to reality.

Oh well, Sarah thought, suddenly realising the time, at least the guests will have the chance to see my paintings without me interfering. Let them form their own impressions before swamping me with all sorts of questions. In any case Sarah rarely knew what to actually tell them about her work, even if she had spent several months on a particular painting.

"You can't explain art," she mumbled under her breath as she tried on a third outfit, a snazzy chequered sleeveless dress that didn't seem quite right. She frowned when she realised most of her wardrobe had slowly piled up on her bed. Don't know why I always spend a fortune on such stunning clothes, seeing that nothing seems to go with anything I own! No wonder I always end up wearing the same tartan miniskirt and black pullover. She swiftly rolled on her black stockings before putting on her favourite combination of clothes that had started to become a kind of uniform for her. Observing herself in the reflection of her bedroom mirror, she smoothed out her skirt. She combed the fringe over her forehead and adjusted her freshly-cut bob, then she pouted her lips and moved her head from one side to the other. *I dread to think what we'd look like if the fashion mafia stopped regurgitating trends from the sixties. Probably awful,* she thought as she laced up her pointy ankle books and put on her leather jacket. It was an unusually chilly evening for summer. Swinging her handbag over her shoulder, she left the house. After locking the front door, she pocketed her keys and trotted down the road.

She drove into the city and parked near the Royal Botanic Gardens before hopping onto a tram. She finally relaxed as it made its way through Melbourne's inner-city suburbs towards the gallery in South Yarra.

"Oh, come and have a look here, Adrian! This one's somewhat unnerving."

"How do you mean, Alistair?"

"It's a bit, well...how should I put it? Um...distressing!"

"Oh, I don't know," he said in disagreement. "On the contrary, I find it rather scintillating."

"Oh no, it's definitely a morbid incursion into the hostile layers of the subconscious mind," Alistair went on. "Why do painters constantly have to keep on raking over unresolved childhood traumas?"

"I admit that there's something openly mysterious in certain parts of it, yet surely not in any negative way. I'm more inclined to think that the artist felt an incandescent faith in life, no matter how rough things turned out to be. Don't you think so?"

"No, neurosis definitely pervades the entire painting."

"Or just your bleak projections!" retorted Adrian. "I don't know why you're being so harsh today. Has something got under your skin? In any case I hope you're not going to tear it to bits and do one of our up-and-coming painters an undue injustice. You'd at least have to extol the brilliant use of amaranthine and ochre."

"Just look more closely at how the paint has been applied! As if it's been brusquely smudged in a state of grim anguish."

"I quite like the painting. I suppose we could simply write two separate reviews of this one," Adrian said in way of compromise.

"And what are all these random dabs and dollops of olive paint?" he asked, thinking he had found another good reason to criticise it.

"Well, I can see you're not going to give it the praise it deserves."

"Perhaps you'll notice a particular form of sublimation under way," began an older academic, "something akin to subduing certain irrepressible instincts…"

"And all along I thought she was basically trying to over-embellish reality by using all these floral motifs," a second academic went on.

"Believe me, it's nothing but a matter of repressed lust."

"Hm, I quite like this one," a woman began eagerly. "Oh, yes, there's definitely something here. Rebecca, come and have a look!"

"Not bad, Rosalyn. I have to agree with you on this one, but just this once, seeing that we have what I call asymmetrically differing tastes," she quipped.

"I'm glad we agree for once. And it's not very often that I see something that I wish was hanging in our living room," she added, still quite awestruck. "I think we should purchase this gem before the artist becomes a household name."

"If it hasn't sold yet," added Rebecca, looking around the gallery's interior for a price list. "We're in luck. Painting number eight: *Lucinda was here* by Sarah Hafner. A real bargain at $850."

"So much?" Rosalyn's eyes widened in disbelief.

"It'll probably be ten times that amount this time next year, so best snap it up before it's worth a fortune," advised her friend.

"And if the artist fades into obscurity, what'll we do with it then?" she asked.

"Continue to admire it, dear," she began. "Don't just see everything as a financial investment."

Although Sarah rarely drank alcohol at her exhibitions, this time she found herself indulging in a second gin and tonic. Perhaps it was Dutch courage, as she knew she might have to face an art critic who didn't exactly have a reputation of being very flattering. However, she had needlessly panicked, for he ended up directing his venom at another artist's work this time. Relieved and in high spirits, she drowned the rest of her glass whilst she caught a glimpse of one of Dorothy's paintings that she was sure would appeal to Eric. As she was about to turn around, she abruptly bumped into Alan of all people.

"Oh Alan, I'm terribly sorry, I didn't see you," she apologised.

"That's alright, no harm done," he said as he helped her regain some balance. "Nice to see you again, Sarah! How's the exhibition going?" he asked eagerly.

"So far so good. I'm still a bit nervous, though, as many art critics are lurking about the place," she said as she let go of Alan's hands to scrutinize the interior of the building.

"Oh, you'll be okay; I think your paintings are wonderful," he said.

"Well, keep your fingers crossed anyway, as some of them can be rather merciless. A lot may depend on their feedback. From all the painters featured today, only two will be chosen to showcase more of their work in another exhibition later on in the year."

"I'm sure you'll be one of them," he said reassuringly.

"If only you could join the judges' panel," she said in a wishful tone. "Listen Alan, since you appear to be in much better shape than me, would you mind driving me home tonight? Or at least to my car, provided I've sobered up by then?"

"With pleasure," Alan said happily.

"Great. Oh look, there's Dorothy, let me introduce you two..."

Sarah had completely entranced Alan, yet he quickly realised she didn't feel quite the same way about him, which was just as well, he thought to himself, as he had a wife and two children at home. Nevertheless, this didn't stop him from admiring the artist in more ways than one. Although there was no way in the world he would even contemplate committing adultery, Alan had a mischievous vein of fantasy to which he would often give free rein...

Forty-nine

Lucinda finally started to paint the Czech countryside, beginning with Milena's village. It had been a while since her first visit, but, as promised, Milena had made fruit dumplings for lunch. Afterwards they decided to walk the dog around the quaint village to absorb the wintry atmosphere. A row of walnut trees leading up to a farmhouse as well as a rusting old plough caught Lucinda's attention. They were lightly covered in snow. While Milena was trying to keep Bobík away from a local Labrador, Lucinda started to make a rough sketch of the idyllic surroundings. After about ten minutes, though, she decided she'd had enough details for a new painting. She hastily shoved her sketchbook back into her bag, and put on her leather gloves.

"Brr! It must be about ten below zero," Lucinda said as she briskly rubbed her nose and ears with her scarf.

"As soon as we get home I'll give you some of my own honey calvados, which will warm you up in no time."

"Can't wait to try it!"

Making homemade schnapps was an illegal 'pastime' that the government more or less turned a blind eye to, simply because they couldn't possibly arrest every third person in the rural parts of the country. Apple, pear, cherry and plum trees abounded, so it was common practice to distil whatever grew on your property.

"Mmh, your 'medicine' is doing me a world of good, Milena," Lucinda affirmed after her second glass. Not only had her cheeks regained their natural colour, she even felt a bit tipsy. "How long do the winters here last, anyway?" she asked Milena.

"Well, it is only mid February, dear, so it'll be a while yet before we start warming up," she said, pouring herself another glass. "In the meantime, we need to use other methods."

Fifty

All had been going well for Eric in Europe. He had presented papers at two conferences in the Czech Republic and given a series of lectures on Australian art at the Masaryk University in Brno, all of which had been well received. He had also met Lucinda of all people. Unknown to him at the time, she had served him a cup of coffee while he was writing a postcard to Sarah on one of his last days in that town. Although they exchanged a few pleasantries, the café was extremely busy that day, so she didn't have time for a proper chat, and Eric still had other things on his mind, such as buying his train ticket to Heidelberg. By the time things quietened down, Lucinda noticed that the seat that Eric had occupied was suddenly empty, and she found herself regretting the fact that they hadn't exchanged phone numbers. Oh well, she thought as she took the empty cup from his table, wondering whether he would ever set foot in her café again. As Eric ambled down Masaryk Avenue, thoughts of the cute waitress and other scattered recollections of his academic holiday filled his mind. Eric couldn't have had a more enjoyable stay. He had escaped the greater part of one of Australia's hottest summers and before returning home he had a conference in Germany to look forward to. As he tossed his postcard into a letterbox near the station, he wondered how Sarah had been spending her time...

Fifty-one

Sarah made sure the heating was turned all the way up. She wasn't used to parading around in nothing but stockings, a miniskirt and a white transparent blouse. As she came closer to Alan, who was lying naked on a thick rug, Dorothy was making sure his outstretched arms were securely tied to the legs of the bed. While Sarah stood there gazing lasciviously into his eyes, she could feel the pleasure he derived from the generous view she granted him from above. She slowly lowered herself towards his face until she was on her knees, which was sending his senses reeling. Breathing in her delicate scent, his eyes widened as she proceeded to lift her skirt. Just as Alan thought Sarah was going to descend even further, she started to unbutton her blouse. Meanwhile Dorothy gently licked and kissed Sarah's erect nipples. He sighed pleasurably as Sarah's left hand held up the front of her skirt while her right hand slowly made its way downwards. It rested between her legs only about ten centimetres away from Alan's parting lips. Sarah then looked deeply into Alan's eyes that glinted lustfully at the sight of her caressing herself.

While Dorothy was taking her clothes off, she wondered what it was that intrigued Alan so much about Sarah. It was possibly her ambiguous and enigmatic nature which was in stark contrast to the way people were in Alan's own predictable little world. Not being able to fathom Sarah's personality probably made her all the more appealing to him. Yet what else was so special about her? For many women were good at drawing attention to themselves not only by the words they used, but also the clothes they wore or the suggestive way they looked at someone. Whatever it was, Alan's mind felt enslaved. Sarah, on the other hand, cared little for rational explanations, for she visibly savoured the power she had over Alan with a wicked fervour.

"Does my body please you?" she asked while she moved her thighs from side to side.

"Oh, yes," Alan replied as his eyes followed her every move.

"Well, you're going to have to be a little more patient," she said teasingly, and started to caress herself once again, averting her gaze this time. She was deliberately holding back to see how far she could go. Of course, she would have liked to lie on top of Alan to enable him to satiate her carnal urges in other ways, but she tried to ignore his presence as she felt her fingers becoming moist. Her pulse quickened.

"Oh please, you're driving me mad," he pleaded, utterly mesmerized.

"Well, maybe just a brief taste wouldn't do any harm," she said before lowering her hand and placing several fingers inside his mouth.

Not being able to fight her libidinous urges any longer, she lowered herself onto his lips to allow his tongue to begin satiating her lust. Seeing Sarah succumbing to her lubricious instincts and Alan's excited state began to arouse Dorothy to no end. Knowing that such amorous adventures didn't last forever, she was determined to make the most of the situation. Suddenly overcome with debauched desire, she greedily grasped his hardness before easing it firmly between her damp inner depths, playfully writhing up and down. Oh, that's nice, Dorothy moaned as she allowed him to fully enter her. I mustn't be tempted to rush things, although Alan's so absorbed in giving Sarah pleasure, it's distracting him from his own rapture. If I'm ever so careful, I'll be able to relish these sensations all the more and possibly even come before he does, she thought selfishly to herself. Fortunately, I'm in total control now, but must be careful not to extract too much nectar; mmh, our minds will soon be showered in ecstatic bliss, and all tensions finally released, just a few more deep thrusts, it won't be long now...

Fifty-two

Shrouded in snow flakes, Eric made his way through the back streets of Heidelberg, wondering how he was going to spend the next two days. He would most probably return to the university and listen to some of the papers being given at the conference. Originally he had planned to deliver a paper on the extent of the influence French impressionism had on the Heidelberg School. Although the organisers had welcomed his proposition and duly confirmed his participation, he had somehow been completely overlooked. This had eventually come to their attention, but since not one participant had cancelled, it was difficult to find a time and an available room. Understandably, Eric wasn't very happy, and all sorts of people started arguing and blaming each another for the situation, but the hullabaloo didn't solve the problem. In the end, Eric was besieged with apologies, for they couldn't slot him in anywhere, neither time-wise nor thematically. They finally offered him a lunchtime session on the final day of the conference, but by that time he would have boarded a plane back to Australia.

Now that's a lovely way to finish my European stay, grumbled Eric as he sank his teeth into a cheese and spinach borek he had just bought from a delicatessen in the Märzgasse to curb the pangs of hunger that had been menacing him since the mix-up at the university. He veered into another lane that was simply called *Plöck*, and walked past several bakeries and various shops, wolfing down his lunch. He soon came across a second-hand store which made him stop and stare. His dejection soon disappeared as he caught sight of a vintage electric semi-acoustic guitar in the window. It was a much sought-after Japanese-made Epiphone from the early eighties. Chewing heartily, he finished the rest of his meal, still eyeing the guitar with keen interest. A bearded man, who didn't take much notice of Eric as he entered the store, was avidly checking the entries on eBay.

"Hello, I'm interested in the old jazz guitar you have in your shop window."

"Really?" began the man, raising his eyebrows from the screen. "It only arrived this morning."

"Then I've come at the right time," replied Eric with a smile.

"I'm afraid you can't test it, as I don't have an amplifier here, but the previous owner assured me that it had been working when he last used it sometime ago. The neck is straight as an arrow. He did mention that the pots sounded a bit scratchy, though, but I'm sure it's nothing that a bit of soldering couldn't fix."

"Not a problem, I'm used to tinkering around with a guitar's insides."

"Then you'd be getting a real bargain at four-hundred euros. The price isn't negotiable."

After scrutinizing the guitar more closely, making sure that there were no other hidden flaws, Eric found that it played like butter despite its age and oxidised strings. So on a whim, he decided to become its new owner.

Walking through the snow-covered streets outside, Eric looked like a professional musician with the battered case at his side. He couldn't help but smile, and for a moment this serendipitous purchase made him forget about the debacle he had endured earlier at the conference. He suddenly remembered a saying by Dr Lee, who had been his Chinese teacher for two semesters at university. This wise man once told the class to never despair in life, since for every misfortune that came your way, three good things would subsequently happen to you. Two more to go, Eric optimistically mused. Although he could hardly put a proper Chinese sentence together any more, he remembered several of Dr Lee's wisdoms. So I wonder if anything else is going to happen today. He smiled in anticipation.

Eric first thought of bringing his prized possession back to the guesthouse he was staying at along the Gaisbergstrasse, and started to head in that direction, but on his way he happened to pass by a congenial café that caught his attention. Looking through the shop front, he saw that there was a vintage racing bike hanging from the ceiling. Strangely, the place seemed to be luring him inside, so after some hesitation, he decided that a hot drink would do him good and so he entered. The heat instantly fogged up his glasses. He took them off with his free hand and made his way to a quiet table. After leaning his guitar carefully against the wall, he hung his coat on one of the pegs. He sat down and while he was rubbing his hands, he noticed a blurry redhead coming his way. Expecting a waitress, he was surprised to see her take a seat at a nearby table, which had an open book and a cup of coffee on it. His glasses were still all steamed up, so he asked the newcomer for a Kleenex in German.

"Sure, I've still got one or two packets," said the kind stranger in perfect English, as she rummaged in her handbag.

"Is my accent so obvious?" he asked, slightly taken aback.

"No, it's fine, but I'm always grateful for any chance to practise my English. Here you are," she said, handing him a packet.

"Oh, but I couldn't possibly take your last tissues," Eric began, "I'll just wait for my glasses to clear up by themselves."

"No, that's alright, there's another packet hidden somewhere in the depths of my handbag," she said with a smile.

"Well if you're sure, thanks!" said Eric, and began wiping his glasses.

The woman picked up her book but couldn't concentrate. "I can see from your clothes and your look that you're probably British," she said to make conversation.

"Australian, actually," he informed her as he put his glasses on. "And you're German, despite the red hair?" Eric asked, trying to contain his sudden surprise at discovering just how attractive she was.

"Correct. But my grandmother is Scottish, so it must have rubbed off."

"You've even got the lovely freckles to match," Eric said admiringly.

"Oh, don't remind me…" she said uncomfortably.

"Please take it as a compliment; I'm fond of them, really! Sorry, if…"

"Well if you put it like that. I'm Astrid, by the way," she said, extending her hand.

"Eric. Pleased to meet you!"

Eric liked the girl instantly; she seemed to have some sort of magnetic appeal to him, whether it was the way her face brightened up every time she began a sentence or simply her body language. Eric found himself unable to resist the positive energy that emanated from her. Of course, some of it was a mask to conceal the nervousness she felt when around people she didn't know so well. Yet, Eric was oblivious to this, seeing that he was beginning to get caught under her spell.

"So what brings an Australian to Heidelberg?"

"I had been planning on giving a paper at an art

conference this week, but unfortunately there was some kind of organisational mishap, so I won't be participating after all."

"That's too bad. What was your talk going to be about?"

"Ever heard of the Heidelberg School art movement?"

"No, but I'm all curious to find out," she said eagerly, cupping her chin in her right hand. "That is, if you'll have me as your audience," she said, her eyes widening a fraction.

"Well, it all started in Melbourne in the late nineteenth century with a group of highly talented painters who were inspired by French impressionism. They were quite avant-garde for their time, but they produced some of our nation's best paintings. Lots of them actually. I'm sure you'd like them, too," he said.

"I'll have to find out more now."

"There's so much on the net, just google the term..."

"I'm afraid," she said interrupting him, "I categorically shun computers and I don't have a smartphone either," she declared, as if she were making a political statement.

"So how do people reach you?" Eric was curious to know.

"It isn't all that hard. Usually people ring me on my landline at home, it even has an answering machine. Or they write me letters like in the good old days."

"How refreshingly retro," began Eric before adding: "I used to be a bit like that. But once I started teaching at university, they gave me a computer and I haven't looked back since."

"How awful!"

"On the contrary, it's rather indispensable, but, to tell you the truth, it's more of a glorified typewriter than anything else. Don't you need one for your work?" Eric asked as a way to find out more about Astrid.

"I used to work in administration, staring at a screen all day. However, after a couple of years I decided my university education was being wasted, so I became a primary school teacher, where life runs at a much slower pace."

"Well as long as you enjoy it, that's the main thing. I know I couldn't put up with screaming kids all day," added Eric.

"You can't imagine how appreciative they are. But I couldn't do it full time, though. I only teach three days a week, so my weekends are twice as long as they used to be, which…" Astrid suddenly hesitated. While she was wondering whether she should reveal more about herself, a waitress entered the café with two large plates covered by glass cake domes that were steamed up from the cold. She noticed Eric and came to his table.

"I'll be with you in a minute," she said hurriedly.

"I'll have whatever cake is hidden in your right hand," Eric said eagerly.

"And I'll take the other one," added Astrid.

"Fine! Two surprise cakes coming up!" she replied. "Anything to drink?"

"A hot chocolate, please. And I mean *really* hot!" requested Eric with emphasis, as more often than not he found that cafés served it lukewarm, which he found totally repugnant.

"We'll do our best, sir."

"Actually, most people come here to drink coffee; it's apparently the best in town," she began. "But anyway, tell me more about this Heidelberg School," said Astrid, managing to turn the attention away from herself.

"Of course, we must have got sidetracked by technology," he said, then thought for a moment. "The painters had a way of depicting the harsh Australian countryside that made it look like paradise, in fact. I guess impressionism does that to reality in some ways. It would be easier to talk about their work if I could show you some examples."

"I'd love to see them."

"Well, I have a book on the subject that I could show you tomorrow if you like," he suggested.

"Tomorrow afternoon I'm actually going to a concert in Mannheim," she replied. "But why don't…"

"Here are your surprise cakes," said the cheerful waitress, suddenly appearing behind the two guests. One extremely hot chocolate, so mind you don't burn your tongue," she joked as she placed the cakes and the drink on their respective tables, before disappearing behind the counter at the end of the café.

"Um, yours looks nice," said Astrid, eyeing Eric's rich chocolate cake. He in turn had his sights on Astrid's Linzer torte.

"Indeed, um…you wouldn't fancy…?" he asked, indicating the cakes.

"Oh, but I would," she readily agreed, and they quickly exchanged the cakes. "Much obliged!"

"Likewise! She must have forgotten which one was which," Eric concluded happily.

"Or she can't distinguish her left from her right," added Astrid.

"Hmm, I hope yours is as delicious as mine," said Eric as he sampled a forkful of the dessert. As he sipped he felt the colour returning to his cheeks. He turned to look out of the window again and was startled to see snowflakes the size of golf balls falling from the sky. He suddenly had the unnerving feeling they were going to be snowed under. Astrid, on the other hand, seemed far from concerned. She probably had some affinity with the prevailing wintry conditions and obviously knew the difference between a spot of inclement weather and a blizzard, he thought to himself. In any case, being trapped in this café with such a charming woman for some time wouldn't be the worst thing that could happen to me, mused Eric cheerfully.

"Looks like an avalanche outside!" Eric said as he turned around to face Astrid again.

"I guess you Australians are used to a very different kind of weather," she quipped. "But it does seem to be snowing with a vengeance today," she added. Yet after seeing the sudden look of concern on Eric's face, she decided to change the subject. "Um, about tomorrow," Astrid began.

"You were saying something about Mannheim," recalled Eric.

"Exactly, but..." she hesitated, "why don't we meet on Sunday? I'm free all day then," she suggested brightly.

"Would love to, but I'll be at the airport; I'm flying back to Australia, you see," said Eric, clearly regretting this fact.

"Oh what a pity," said Astrid. "Look, if you're not going to spend the whole day packing, why don't you come along with me to the concert? It's a piano recital by a promising Turkish pianist who's made quite a name for herself."

"Sounds tempting. But will there still be tickets available?" he enquired.

"You won't be needing one," she began as her right hand dived into her handbag once again. She fished out two tickets from an envelope. "Ta-da!" she proclaimed, and handed one to Eric.

"Your handbag contains all sorts of surprises! So, whose place am I taking?"

"My former boyfriend's no longer coming along. I'd bought the tickets long before we broke up," she explained.

"What if he shows up anyway?"

"I doubt it. We haven't spoken to each other for months, and he was never really keen on classical music."

"Oh well, his loss, uh...in more ways than one."

"Looking back, I think he only ever came along just to

spite me; I mean, it wasn't as if I had ever coaxed him into joining me."

"It's not healthy when couples do everything together anyway," said Eric, not really knowing what else to say.

"Well it was all rather complex, but in a nutshell, I think we just ran out of things to say to each other."

"That normally happens when you reach the final chapter of a relationship," said Eric emphatically.

"That would about sum it up. And how about you? Don't you have a nice young lady waiting for you back in Melbourne?"

"Well...sort of," he half admitted. "But we never really had the chance of getting to know one another properly."

"You never know; maybe things are just on hold until a more opportune moment turns up."

"You may be right, but I'll cross that bridge when I get to it. Yet in the meantime it would be a pleasure to accompany you to that concert."

"In that case, don't you even want to know what's on the programme?"

"Well as long as it's nothing by Wagner or anything modern and experimental, I really don't mind," he said.

"Then it's a date. But don't think I'm going to tell you what she'll be playing now!" she said, finishing the last of her cake.

"Good, I love surprises!"

"Shall we meet a bit earlier? Then you could tell me more about those Australian painters."

"Gladly, then at least all my preparations for the conference wouldn't have been in vain."

After paying for their afternoon treats, they then swapped telephone numbers and agreed to meet at the station at 4pm the next day. He also made a mental note of coming back to the café first thing in the morning to try their famous coffee.

Fifty-three

"This isn't your autobiography, Bedřich, you've written a far-fetched spy story!" Sarah said as George was serving her tea.

"Well, I did warn you that it contained a few secrets," George said defensively.

"I had to reread most of the passages twice to make sure my eyes weren't playing tricks on me," Sarah said, but started to worry when she saw that his demeanour hadn't changed. "Please, tell me it's just your wild fantasy at play!" she almost pleaded.

"I'm afraid not, my child."

"Oh my God! And in all that time didn't anyone suspect you of leading a double life?"

"No one was allowed to suspect anything about my role in the secret service," he stressed.

"Not even your wife?"

"Especially my wife. I doubt whether she had the slightest suspicion that anything was other than normal," he began. "And I'd like to keep it that way, please."

"Mum's the word," Sarah promised.

"As long as she's still alive, please keep it all to yourself. After that you can have it published or turn it into a spy novel as you call it," he suggested.

"Wouldn't that get me into trouble?" she asked, suddenly worried.

"Well, you'd definitely have to change a few details and not mention anything that happened after I had come to Australia," he informed her.

"Why's that?"

"Well, you see, everything has to be kept silent for a minimum of sixty years; that's standard procedure," he went on. "You already know what I went through in Czechoslovakia, but there are still a few other things I need to tell you about."

"Um," she interrupted him, "I noticed you never mentioned the surname of that Irma woman you had an affair with. You don't remember it by any chance, do you?"

"I remember it very well, it was Beranová. Why do you ask?"

"It's just that I grew up with a girl called Lucinda whose grandmother was called Irma Haluška. But I have no idea about her maiden name."

"There's probably a multitude of women called Irma in the UK, and besides, you were brought up in Devon, whereas my Irma lived in London."

"When you left her she did, but do you have any idea where she went from there?"

"None whatsoever. And with me being in Australia it wasn't as easy to stay in touch as it is nowadays, Sarah, but I think it was better that way."

"Didn't you miss her at all, especially after all you two had gone through together?"

"Immensely at first, but with a wife and son in Australia, I had to suppress such feelings, as I was quite keen to become a part of their life once again. I know my extramarital affair was hardly what you'd consider normal, but my line of work simply defied the conventions and laws of society."

"And morality," she added.

"I don't deny it, nor am I particularly proud of my actions. And perhaps writing this diary will help alleviate the guilt that's been gnawing at my conscience for so long," he explained.

"Don't you ever wonder what became of her? I mean, wouldn't it be exciting to meet up after all this time?"

"Best to let sleeping dogs lie, I always say. She may not have forgiven me for leaving her alone in England, and even assuming she's still alive, there's scant chance of finding her now."

"You never know, Granddad. Life unfolds in the most improbable of ways at times," she said, and suddenly thought about Eric and what he was possibly up to in Europe.

Fifty-four

"**D**idn't I say you would enjoy it?" Astrid smiled.

"It was marvellous, and it also marks the end of my ignorance of this great composer's work," admitted Eric.

"Well, it's not your fault. Although Janáček was a genius, he is probably classical music's best-kept secret," Astrid explained. "And even if you had stumbled upon his other works before, they are an acquired taste."

"I think I'd like to hear more to acquire the taste," Eric said to please her.

"Good, then we'll go back to my place so that you can discover his string quartets," Astrid proposed.

"I don't think I have that much time. Remember I've got a plane to catch tomorrow."

"Oh you needn't worry, he only wrote two. Well, a third one was recently unearthed, eighty years after his death, but it's yet to be recorded."

The piano notes were still resounding in Eric's head as they made their way through the thick snow towards the station. Mannheim's streets were quite confusing to newcomers, for their names were simply made up of letters and numbers. Astrid tried in vain to explain the logic behind this system to Eric, who was happy just to follow her in the same direction as they had come. Of course, it all looked different at night with only the lanterns reminding him of places they had passed, such as the park with the Friedrich Schiller statue in one corner. They stopped in front of the huge greenish bronze figure that stared proudly into the distance while snowflakes continued to fall to the ground, burying everything in thick white layers. Astrid started to hum one of the pieces they had heard that evening.

"Amazing! You've read my thoughts," Eric began.

"It's the fourth piece, *The Frýdek Madonna* I think it was called."

"That's the one; funny how that piece has managed to squeeze the memory of the others out of my mind."

"Yeah, it is quite catchy," agreed Astrid. "Shall we dance?"

"With pleasure, but I'm a hopeless dancer," he warned. "The only thing I ever learned was how to waltz, and badly at that," Eric admitted humbly. "So, my apologies in case I step on your toes!"

"Same here," she said and took his hands. They improvised a waltz around the statue to the tune of their favourite piece.

"Hey, I can't see where I'm stepping with all this snow," Eric said as a way of excuse in case he really did tread on Astrid's shoes.

"We're going to have to stop anyway, I'm becoming rather dizzy," she said, not letting go of Eric's hands. Astrid feigned a surprised look as their eyes met for what seemed like an eternity before they drew each other closer. Whilst Eric's arms suddenly fell to rest around Astrid's waist, she threw her arms around him and they started kissing passionately. Her exhilaration soon turned to laughter, though, when she opened her eyes and saw the snow on Eric's eyelashes, hair and shoulders.

"You're turning into a snowman," she said, wiping off the flakes with her hands.

"Thanks for a lovely evening," he said as they slowly continued their way.

"You're welcome, but it's not over yet. Feel like sharing a pizza with me? I'm famished!"

"Splendid idea," he agreed. "I'm feeling a bit peckish myself."

"Well, there's a little Italian restaurant somewhere near here; I just hope I'll be able to find it again. It has a wonderful homely atmosphere, and the food isn't bad either."

"I'm all for it."

Holding hands, they ventured through the geometric town centre (all the streets were straight and flat in Mannheim similar to a Monopoly board) until they found the place a short while later. Three or four lively Italian families were conversing amiably and, of course, eating copiously. Astrid and Eric took seats at the only free table and quickly felt at home. After their meal, they caught the train back to Heidelberg and headed for Astrid's flat, which was in the suburb of Handschuhsheim. Her street resembled a Swiss ski resort. Seeing that it continued to snow heavily, no one had bothered to sweep away the snow and ice off the pavement, which was a legal obligation throughout Germany.

"I just love to hear the sound of the snow crunching under our boots," Astrid said as they reached the front door. "I live on the top floor," she said as they entered.

"That must keep you fit," Eric commented as he followed her up.

"I'll make us a lovely cup of hot cocoa to warm us up," she said as they clomped up the stairs.

"How could I refuse such an enticing offer?"

"You can't! Anyway we've got to make the most of your last evening in Europe, although I wonder…" she began.

"I really wish there were some way I could stay a bit

longer; I'm missing you already," Eric declared sadly.

"Hm, it wouldn't surprise me, though, if there weren't any planes flying at all," she speculated.

"Is there any way of finding out?"

"Haven't you checked? I mean, you still have to check in, don't you?" she asked as she unlocked her door.

"Well, I can only do an online check-in twenty-four hours before my flight, so actually now would be an ideal time, but seeing you don't have a computer..."

After they had taken off their boots, scarves, gloves and coats, Astrid grabbed Eric's hand and led him to the sofa where they started to kiss once again.

"Hmm, stay here with me, at least for a couple more days," she said in between kisses. "Perhaps the runways have turned into ice-rinks and they're all snowed under."

"Wishful thinking!"

"But not so unlikely, considering the circumstances," she continued.

"In any case, best check before I head to the airport tomorrow," Eric said as he went to fetch his phone from his coat. "Oh, the airline people have sent me a message... 'Flight postponed until further notice due to adverse weather conditions. We apologise for any inconvenience and will keep you informed.' Oh dear!" He stopped reading and gave Astrid a concerned look. "Our wish seems to have come true."

"Well, I may as well go and make us some hot cocoa now," she said and left the room.

"I'll be right with you," Eric said before reading a few more messages he had missed that day. He then got up, shrugged his shoulders and made his way into the kitchen. Astrid was busy stirring the milk while she added several heaped teaspoons of cocoa. Hot steam was already beginning to form.

"Mmm, smells good!" Eric approved.

"Timing is the key. When making really hot chocolate, you mustn't allow the milk to scald and form a horrible layer of skin," she began, whilst briefly turning around to smile at Eric.

"Oh, definitely. I couldn't think of anything more ghastly," he said in an exaggerated tone before coming close behind Astrid to look over her shoulders.

"It's difficult to prevent the skin from forming when it's being heated," she said, suddenly finding it hard to concentrate, seeing that Eric had started to kiss the nape of her neck. "Therefore you need to keep on stirring to break up the fat molecules…" Eric continued kissing her, this time on her lips whilst his right hand gently moved up and down her back before settling upon her behind. With her eyes firmly fixed on the pot, Astrid did her best to stir the cocoa. Excitement started to overwhelm her, for she had no way of anticipating Eric's next move. "Um…if the protein and fat molecules are allowed to form clumps…hmm…oh, please stop. Don't you realise that dreaded skin will appear on the milk's surface once those molecules start to evaporate," she pleaded unconvincingly as Eric's hands managed to lift her skirt while he was rubbing his body against hers. Without taking her eyes off the pot, Astrid moaned discreetly. All along Astrid still managed to stir the hot beverage while she allowed Eric to caress her between her thighs. "This is full-cream milk, Eric. That means the proteins are soon going to bond with the fat and once they dry and evaporate…" After he had removed his trousers, Eric slowly started to remove Astrid's stockings. She voluntarily bowed towards the stove with her elbows supporting her against the kitchen bench. "You mustn't do anything silly now, otherwise our hot chocolate's doomed," she said in a tone that seemed to encourage Eric even further as she parted her taut legs.

They began making passionate love. Not really being able to stir any more, Astrid had nevertheless managed to turn off the stove, fearing that the milk could boil over any minute. She moved into a less awkward position as Eric continued his thrusting movements, which only intensified her pleasure. He relished watching Astrid succumb to unbridled lust. Suddenly grabbing Eric's thighs, Astrid pushed Eric deeper inside her as she climaxed in quivering spasms. Their mutual fluids streamed down Astrid's legs as they slowly detached their bodies from one another. They then both collapsed to the floor next to the oven, still breathing heavily.

"Mmm, that was nice," Eric said after quite a while. His mind felt blissfully empty.

"I'm all shaky," Astrid said as she lifted herself off the floor. "How I needed that!" she concluded, looking at Eric for the first time since he entered the kitchen. She collected her clothes and left for the bathroom.

Eric also got to his feet and laughed when he noticed that an unappetizing layer of skin had formed on the cocoa's surface. With the help of a teaspoon, he skimmed it off, and turned on the stove to medium heat. "Here we go again," he whispered to himself and started stirring vigorously.

Fifty-five

"Would you care for another cup," George asked as he noticed his granddaughter playing with the handle of her empty cup.

"Just a drop, thanks."

"There you go," he said as he poured her the rest of the tea.

"Was your life ever in danger?"

"A couple of times. But I haven't come to that bit yet in my memoirs."

"Have you ever, um…" Sarah began, yet hesitated somewhat at the thought of such an unpleasant subject, "killed anyone?"

"God has luckily spared me of such a necessity. But Irma once came close to taking someone's life," he added.

"Really?" Sarah asked.

"Well, it was in order to save mine."

"How did that happen?"

"It was just before we left the country. My superiors had asked me to exchange some information with a Czech spy called *Magor* whom a colleague of mine Robin was in the process of converting. We were also keen on having a mole, you see. In hindsight, it all seemed too good to be true. He appeared so trustworthy, but he turned out to be an exceptionally good actor instead. On this occasion he was supplying me with the names of several influential Party members who would soon be working at their Embassy in London, together with invaluable information about their intentions to further infiltrate our ministries. All had gone well, and the next day Irma and I had planned on leaving the country. Robin must have either mentioned something in passing, possibly without even realising it, but it was clear that he had let on that we were departing for good, as I was awoken by knocks at the door at around eight o'clock the next morning. Thinking at first that it must have been Irma who had gone out to fetch us some breakfast, I got out of bed, still muzzy from sleep, and opened the front door. To my surprise it wasn't Irma, but Magor standing in the doorway with a gun pointing directly at me."

"Oh my God!" exclaimed Sarah.

"Well, I wasn't too thrilled about it either, especially when I thought we could trust this chap. Anyway, he ordered me to go to the window and open it. He told me that apart from the fact that I knew too much, they needed a scapegoat for Blanka's death to make it look as if we were responsible. Therefore, he was first going to get rid of me before taking care of Robin. That way, he would prevent any information whatsoever from leaking out and become a socialist hero in the process."

"How despicable! Poor Bedřich," Sarah said empathetically.

"So you can imagine how terrified I was, expecting him to shoot me any minute…"

"And where was Irma then?"

"I assumed they had arrested her or taken her away for questioning, but all along she had been in the bathroom painting her toenails of all things."

"And then?" Sarah asked impatiently.

"Magor made me sit on the ledge and lean backwards.

Then he pressed his gun against my chest and started pushing."

"That window must have been huge," she said.

"Well wide enough to accommodate me," George began. "I tried talking to him to gain some time, but from the deranged look in his eyes I realised there was no way I was going to be able to reason with him. Then just as I thought I was about to draw my last breath, Irma suddenly walked into the room. To distract Magor, I screamed 'Look out!' to make him think I was bluffing, and to help drown out the sound of her footsteps. Luckily, he didn't turn around, and Irma, instead of panicking, instinctively grabbed the heavy ceramic flowerpot next to her and swiftly smashed it over his head."

"Rather quick-witted, wasn't she?" Sarah said in admiration.

"I'll say! Otherwise there would have been another defenestration in Czechoslovakia! Anyway, our double agent instantly fell to the ground, dropping his gun. She had knocked him out cold. There were broken fragments of the pot everywhere. I was so relieved that I couldn't stop hugging her."

"Your guardian angels were working overtime that day," she said, wide-eyed. "What did you do then? Was he still alive?"

"His heart was still beating, but we weren't going to take any chances, so I called Robin to come over and help us. He injected him with a strong tranquillizer that would keep him heavily sedated for the whole day, and I poured some whisky into his mouth and all over his clothes, and brought him down to reception, telling the concierge we had discovered a drunk lying in the corridor."

"That was terribly clever of you!"

"Well, it seemed a shame to waste my only bottle of

Bruichladdich on that thug, but we had no choice."

"Ingenious."

"We couldn't pat ourselves on the back yet, as we still had a lot to take care of, so we packed our bags and made our way by bus to the Austrian border via a small town called Mikulov."

"Did they suspect anything?"

"Fortunately not. It was a Saturday. They checked our passports, saw that I had a working visa and just assumed we were a nice English couple going on a day trip. The boys had done such a great job on Irma's passport, even forging a fictitious date of arrival based on the stamp I had received."

"Amazing! So how was Vienna?"

"We had a lovely time," George began and blushed a little. "My boss informed me that they would send us plane tickets by Monday, so we spent the weekend sightseeing and trying to avoid thinking about our imminent separation." He left the room to make some more tea. "Another cup, Sarah?" he called out loudly.

"Oh, no thanks, I'm fine," she said, but wanted to know more. "How did Irma feel about being in the West?"

"Understandably, it was all too much for her. On the plane she couldn't stop crying, so much did she miss her family, but I promised her my successor would contact them. Other than that, she felt terribly nauseous during the first few days."

"She wasn't pregnant by any chance, was she?"

"That also crossed my mind, but she stoutly denied it."

"That must have been a relief for both of you," Sarah said, trying hard to imagine their predicament.

"She was also a very good actress," he added and sipped his tea. But before Sarah could start wondering what he meant by this, he quickly changed the subject. "In any case, I let her stay in my flat until I was ordered to emigrate for good. We had already bent the rules a few too many times, and before anyone became suspicious, they thought it best to reunite me with my family, where I could also be of further use to them."

"How considerate of them," she said cynically, but was too curious about other things to worry about blaming anyone for ruining relationships. "Tell me more about your last year in Britain, Granddad."

"At first it was all quite hectic. Settling into a new way of life and being interrogated by our lads was all a bit too much for poor Irma. Somehow she began to fear for her life."

"Whatever for?"

"She suspected that Blanka's death was not kosher, no matter what they or I had tried to tell her about Magor's confession that the STB had killed her. So to secure her own safety, she had put her diary together with another statement supposedly containing the name of the mole into a bank vault as a precaution to be made public if anything should happen to her."

"Now that was clever of her," Sarah began. "But, hang on, if something had happened to her, who would have actually opened the vault, you being in Australia? And how do you know that they didn't double-cross her in the end?"

"Whether or not they guessed that she was probably bluffing didn't really matter. At that point the mole had already been found, so they gave her to understand that nothing at all would happen to her as long as the information regarding the mole's existence remained secret for the next sixty years. That was the proviso she has had to live with until...well, this...or last year, in fact."

"How did she react?"

"She became irrational and even wanted to throw away the key to the safe forever, but I convinced her to keep it, as she had also deposited other valuables that she might need one day. She nevertheless told me the code for safekeeping in the event that she ever forgot it. Everything's probably still there locked up in one of the vaults."

"Let's try to find her! I mean, it can't be that hard. All we have to do is find an eighty-five year old lady called Irma, née Beranová, n'est-ce pas?"

"Your optimism is adorable, Sarah," George said, and then sighed. "She's probably living off the very pension she was promised for her services to the country."

"Terrible how time flies."

Fifty-six

Melbourne, 16th March 2016

Dear Astrid,

Hope you are well! To my shame I have to admit that I haven't finished reading your book yet. Not that it had ceased to captivate me in any way, but exhaustion simply lulled me into a deep sleep after we had taken off. Actually my boarding pass is still sandwiched between one of Janáček's most intimate letters to his beloved muse. Talk about unrequited love! I promise I'll send it back to you as soon as I've read it.

I have since got over my dismay at having been excluded from participating in last month's conference in your city, although admittedly, I did grumble more than I normally do, as such academic events are few and far between. An invitation to a future conference has yet to make an appearance in my letterbox. In the interim I have forgiven and almost forgotten, for had it all not turned out the way it did, I doubt whether I would have strayed into that cosy café, and then we would never have met...

Back home again, most of the impressions gathered on my European trip have slowly given way to the realities of timetables, teaching and the forthcoming football season! Only you and the short time we had spent together seem to have left an indelible impression in my memory. I'm seriously considering taking a sabbatical and coming to Heidelberg, yet it may already be too late for this year. I don't suppose you'd consider coming to Australia for a while, would you?

Greetings and kisses from a sunburnt country,
Eric

Fifty-seven

During the Easter holidays, Karel, Lucinda, her parents and Veronika all went to visit Irma to celebrate her eighty-sixth birthday. For her age she was quite a sprightly woman intent on enjoying her life as long as she could.

Irma and Lucinda soon found themselves alone in the kitchen.

"It's so nice to see you again, Lucinda!" said Irma brightly. "Your stay abroad seems to have done you a world of good."

"I needed it badly. I had started to age beyond my years."

"Well, while you're still blessed with enchanting looks," began Irma, "you should wear more jewellery. I have some garnet necklaces and earrings as well as some golden rings that I'd like to give you."

"That's sweet of you, dear Irma, but why don't you keep them?"

"Look, I haven't worn them in years, so why bother now when I'm old and haggard."

"Oh Irma, please! I'm sure they would suit you just as they did in the past."

"You'll be inheriting them from me anyway, but you needn't wait till I'm pushing up daisies. So you're going to have them now, and that's that!"

"If you insist, I'll gladly accept them."

"Only thing is that I've got them all locked up in a safety box in a vault at Barclay's bank on Park Lane," she revealed.

"In London?"

"That's right. I lived there for a few years after I had arrived in Britain back in the fifties," she explained before taking out an object from a drawer of her desk. "This is the key you'll need to access it. I thought it was lost for good until I recently found it whilst doing a spot of spring cleaning."

"Will it still be valid after all these years?"

"Of course, dear. There may be one or two other minor things, but they can stay in there."

Seeing that Lucinda and Karel had to go to London to catch their late-afternoon flight to Brno, they took an early train in order to have enough time to go to the bank and recover the jewellery.

Since they were the only customers intending to clear out a safety deposit box that day, it wasn't long before a friendly bank official showed them the way to the inner depths of the old building. After descending several flights of stairs, they entered the womb-like interior of the bank's vaults, where hundreds of safety boxes were stored side by side. Lucinda felt quite excited as they found themselves in front of Irma's.

"Now, if you'll just enter the code here, you'll be able to access the box with your key," the man instructed.

"What code?" asked Lucinda, becoming uneasy.

"Each box can only be accessed by both a code word and a key."

"My grandmother never mentioned anything about a code; she only gave me this key," Lucinda said, suddenly taken aback.

"Then I'm afraid you're going to have to ask her for the

accompanying code as well. The system won't allow you to use your key otherwise."

"Oh well, there's nothing for it, we'll just have to leave it for next time," Karel said realistically.

"That's too bad," she said, quite disheartened. "Sorry for wasting your time," she apologised to the patient bank official.

"No need to worry; the contents aren't going anywhere," he assured her.

"It's not that I'm worried about," Lucinda began. "It's my grandmother's memory that bothers me."

"Why don't we just ring her before we head for the airport?" Karel suggested as they made their way up the stairs of the bank.

"Code?"

"Yes, Gran, you apparently left behind some kind of code word, and we can't open the safety box without it," Lucinda said into the phone. There was a long silence, as Irma gathered her thoughts. Vague long-suppressed memories of the past started to fill her mind.

"Oh dear, I really can't remember, but...a man I used to know a long time ago probably does," she said solemnly.

"Is there any way of contacting him?" Lucinda asked.

"Well, I don't know, dear," Irma began. "He emigrated to Australia in the early fifties and we haven't been in touch since," she went on. "He may not even be alive, for all I know."

"Hang on, Irma. This man wouldn't happen to be *Colin Wood*, would he?"

"Uh... How on earth did you know about him?" Irma said after another awkward silence.

"He was mentioned in the diary that your sister let me read when I visited her. It contained quite a few intriguing things about your past, yet nothing about your time in the UK."

"I had totally forgotten about that diary. Now I recall that I left it back home for my relatives. Actually, it's probably just as well that you couldn't open the safety deposit box after all," she concluded nervously.

"Why not, Irma?"

"There's another diary in there, as well as one or two things that still need to be kept secret."

"Now I'm all curious, Gran."

"It's a shame about the jewellery, and I'm terribly sorry you went all that way for nothing," she said apologetically.

"It's alright, Gran. It was on our way to the airport anyway."

"Look, when your sabbatical's over I'll buy you some other jewellery to make it up to you."

"Oh Gran, you needn't do that."

"I insist, dear. I promised you necklaces and earrings and you shall have them!"

Oh well, it just wasn't meant to be, thought Lucinda as she hung up the receiver after her conversation with Irma. Easy come, easy go!

Fifty-eight

Heidelberg, 8th April 2016

Dear Eric,

I hope it was only the country that was sunburnt and not you! Although spring is just around the corner here, it still feels as though Germany has become a part of the Arctic zone.

I have to admit that once you had boarded your plane, I felt depressed and then came the withdrawal symptoms. Fortunately, the routines of existence soon started to fill the emptiness your absence had created.

I am a creature of the present moment, Eric – always have been and probably always will be. I was never one to reminisce or look forward to a faraway future. And above all I have no right to wrest you away from your established life, whether now or in a year's time. Such a period would no doubt create a greater void between us. Sorry to sound so rational and unromantic, but I've been through such 'relationships' before, which regretfully all turned out to be affairs without any perspective. And experience has taught me time and time again that there's no such thing as living 'happily ever after', which is the main reason I'd like to keep the memories of our marvellous encounter exactly as they are.

I'm not as emotionally disciplined as you appear to be, Eric. Please forgive me. I know we shared some magical moments, but it's time for both of us to cross other bridges.

Astrid
P.S. Oh and please keep the book as a souvenir.

Fifty-nine

After much searching, Sarah's mother was finally able to find the address of Lucinda's parents. Fifteen years had elapsed since Sarah had last written to her childhood friend, so she knew it was going to be a rather long letter. Seven pages later, she thought she had just about exhausted her long-term memory. Although she did mention the fact that she was currently helping her grandfather write his memoirs, she didn't go into any detail about his secret life other than to ask Lucinda whether by any chance 'Beranová' had been her grandmother's maiden name.

Sixty

Back in Brno, Lucinda immersed herself in her painting, and all thoughts of Irma's past, her jewellery and other secrets, which were probably going to be locked up forever, were cast away to the back of her mind. She thought she had done all she could to unravel the mysteries that the sands of time were going to bury yet again.

To cheer Lucinda up, Kamila had taken her to see a string quartet perform.

"I really like the pieces we just heard, although I'm not familiar with George Onslow's work," Lucinda admitted guiltily, "so you'll have to excuse my ignorance."

"Don't worry, I bet most people here tonight don't know much about him either, but perhaps you've heard of the next composer," Kamila said, giving her a questioning look.

"Alfred Hill? No, can't say I have unfortunately," Lucinda said, biting her lower lip.

"He was a popular Australian composer in the late nineteenth century," Kamila said, which immediately made Lucinda think of Sarah. She wondered if she would ever hear from her again. Little did she know that Sarah's letter was already on its way to her parents' letterbox.

Sixty-one

Sarah and Dorothy ended up being featured in a combined exhibition as the two new outstanding artist discoveries of the year. Sarah not only felt exalted but relieved. She was on her way to achieving what she had long been striving for.

After having mingled with the crowd, Sarah exchanged a few words with several guests before being overcome by a strange sense of déjà vu.

Without knowing exactly why or how, she started to walk in the direction of a man standing alone in one corner admiring one of Dorothy's paintings. She suddenly found herself standing behind Eric. She waited for him to turn around, and without saying a single word they lunged at each other and started kissing to the complete surprise of the guests standing nearby.

"Nothing's changed," said Sarah, shaking her head.

"I knew we'd end up together," said Eric dreamily.

"I was referring to your preference for Dorothy's paintings!"

"But it's you I want in my arms."

"In that case I'll overlook your artistic taste," she said before kissing him again.

This proved to both of them that their encounter prior to Eric's European trip hadn't just been an infatuation (as in Astrid's case) but a sign of what was to come. This time, Sarah was sure their love would blossom and become a part of their everyday lives.

Sixty-two

While Irma was watering her plants, there was a sudden clap of thunder outside. Seeing that the windows were wide open, the noise startled her so much that she knocked over one of her earthenware flowerpots. Oh bother, she thought, and frowned. As she started to pick up the broken pieces, she was suddenly transported back in time. Vivid images began to form of a man sprawled out on the floor in front of her after the blow she had given him with the heavy flowerpot. She then saw herself in the arms of the man whose life she had just saved.

Another clap of thunder brought Irma out of her reverie while she cleared away the soil that was lying on one of her favourite rugs. Whatever became of George, she wondered. Not even a period of sixty years could erase him from her memory.

Sixty-three

"So what was Australia like in the fifties, Bedřich?" Sarah asked her grandfather.

"It was full of communists and Czech spies," he lamented, "but apart from that it was a marvellous place."

"It kept you busy, I imagine."

"Right up until the seventies," he began. "After that the secret service didn't really know what to do with me. I sort of became redundant, so they just let me teach full time, and that was that," he concluded.

"So we've still got some more pages to fill, haven't we?"

"Well, for the time being, we're finished. Everything else has to be kept secret for another decade, I'm afraid."

"Even if I promise not to tell a soul?"

"Well, maybe just a few details wouldn't do any harm, I suppose."

"I'm all ears!"

Sixty-four

Even though Eric had been able to demystify many aspects of Sarah's complex being, she was still an enigma to him. While one minute she was spontaneous, devilishly playful or even exuding an air of seductiveness, the next she could be inexplicably aloof from everything happening around her, not just when she was standing in front of her easel, but also in Eric's presence. Her ambiguous nature both perplexed and delighted Eric, casting an enduring spell on him.

She's in one of her contradictory moods again, Eric realised, but decided not to leave her on her own.

Sarah stared at the blank canvas and sighed. She was disheartened.

"What's wrong?" Eric asked as he came into the room looking rather cheerful.

"No inspiration today!" she complained, whipping the canvas angrily with her paintbrush.

"Then why don't you come with me to the footy?" he suggested.

"To the football?" she asked, giving him an incredulous look.

"Why not?"

"And you think watching a bunch of grown men frantically running after an egg-shaped ball is going to inspire me?"

"Who knows? Maybe you'll see things in a new light."

"Hm," she reflected, looking at the canvas. "You could be right though." Sarah shrugged after a brief frown. "Perhaps I just need to get away from myself for a while," she surmised and flung her paint brush into the water jar.

"Then get dressed, there's a train leaving in half an hour. Oh, and wear something in blue and white, if possible!"

Walking out of Flinders Street Station, Sarah always stopped and wondered which of the nine clocks she was standing under. She would then try to guess the name of the respective train line.

"Sandringham!" she said aloud, before turning her head around towards the clock above her.

"Drat! Williamstown line."

"What's with you?" Eric asked, wondering what she was on about.

"Wrong clock again!" she replied grumpily.

"Oh well, there's always next time," he said, realising this was just another one of her little idiosyncrasies. "C'mon, there's our tram. We'll miss the beginning of the match if we don't hurry up!"

"I have to admit it's quite enjoyable, but I couldn't do it every weekend."

"It's a nice ritual, I find."

"It's more like a national religion," Sarah stated, observing the delirious crowds around them.

"Yeah, you could see it that way, I suppose," Eric said, his eyes glued to the field.

"I like that nimble player, number twenty-nine," Sarah said, trying to show some enthusiasm for a game whose rules she still didn't fully understand.

"That's Brent Harvey; he's played more games than any other footballer in history," he said in admiration.

"He looks like he knows what he's doing. No one seems to be able to catch him when he's got the ball," she observed.

"He's quite a legend."

"Look there he goes again, he…" Sarah began, but her words were drowned by the loud roar from half the crowd in the stadium. "I guess that must have been a goal," she said as the noise slowly subsided.

"It certainly was!"

Sixty-five

Brno, 10th August 2016

Dear Sarah,

You can't believe how happy I was to receive your letter, especially after all these years. It took some time to reach my parents though (probably thanks to some rigorous tracing feats), since they have long since moved out of the old house that you knew as a girl. When we last corresponded, you had just begun your studies, and here you are embarking on a career as a painter! At least one of us has managed to live out their dreams. I still paint myself, but only as a way to relax and switch off.

It's incredible how similar our paths in life have been. Whereas you gave up teaching after seven years, it took me almost ten just to dare take a year off. I guess it's my neurotic need for security that doesn't allow me to break away completely. My sabbatical year is almost over – I've been spending it in my ancestral Brno, where, amongst other things, I've been unearthing juicy details about my grandmother's past. If only you knew what she'd been through before coming to the UK! Thanks for enquiring about sweet old Irma (her maiden name was indeed Beranová. How on earth did you know that?) In any case, she's still as adorable as ever. She recently wanted to give me her jewellery and other things that she has stashed away in a safety deposit box in London. So Karel (the new love of my life) and I went all the way there with the key she'd given me, but we were denied access, as I didn't have the code word that was required. Some long-lost friend of hers apparently has it, but the last time she saw him was in the fifties, so it looks as if everything will be locked up in that bank forever and ever, amen!

And now I'm back in Brno, keeping busy as Karel's assistant. He has made quite a name for himself as a photographer. I'll be here for another month, though, as that's when my sabbatical year ends. It would be really lovely to see you again. If you haven't made any plans for summer (I mean, your winter, of course), you're welcome to come over and visit me. I'd also love to visit the land of the kangaroos one day. Yet in the interim say hello to your folks from me, and please write soon.

Take care,
Lucinda

Sixty-six

"Not long ago you told me that Irma had given you the password to her safe in the vault. You don't by any chance still remember it, do you?" Sarah asked her grandfather hopefully.

"Of course I do," he said, "the code was *Šárka*."

"Now that name rings a bell!"

"Yes, it's the name of my favourite symphonic poem from Smetana's 'Má vlast'," George said, thinking that Sarah knew this for a fact.

"Now everything makes sense!"

"Does it?" He gave her a perplexed look.

Sarah just smiled without answering.

Sixty-seven

Images of the man Irma had once loved and whose baby she had brought into this world seemed to be resurfacing involuntarily. All in all, she was glad she had never stood in the way of his own wife and child all those years ago. The man who eventually married Irma not long after George had left for Australia, accepted her first child as if it were his own, so much was he in love with her. A serendipitous encounter had brought the two together. It was an extraordinarily windy day, and while Irma was walking along the Thames and feeling rather despondent, her beret suddenly flew from her head, past the crowds of people behind her, and finally into the hands of Thomas Haluška, just centimetres away from the water's edge. It had also started to rain, so he offered her the shelter of his umbrella until they arrived at a café where she thought it only fitting to invite this charming man for a cup of tea. They exchanged stories of how they had come to England in the first place. Whilst he had nothing to hide (he was a Slovakian journalist who had decided to stay on after the war), she gave him a more benign version of her torrid adventures. He became totally infatuated with Irma and the two married before Šárka (Lucinda's mother) was born. A year later they had a second child, Veronika. Then they both found work in Exeter. Although Thomas was fifteen years older than Irma, they had a harmonious relationship until he died at the age of ninety. Never once had they spoken about Šárka's father, so she really felt all memory of George had been more or less eradicated from her mind.

Sixty-eight

Sarah jumped at the opportunity to see her old childhood friend again. At her insistence, Eric came along, even if somewhat reluctantly at first, seeing that he had practically only come back from Europe seven months earlier. But he had four weeks off, so he happily acquiesced. Sarah and Lucinda's reunion was like dreaming while one was awake. As an onlooker, Eric couldn't help but marvel at how life was able to unfold at times.

Epilogue

Sarah was sitting on the plane back to Australia after spending three weeks in Britain. She was holding Eric's hand while he peacefully slept beside her. She wasn't used to flying such long distances, so she felt uneasy and found herself wide awake.

I still can't believe all that happened, she thought. After all this time, how the tears flowed when we finally saw each other. Fifteen years, so significant in human terms, but just a drop in the ocean of time. It's a wonder I never thought of visiting my home town before, she pondered, realising for the first time how little she knew about Europe. Apart from the few times she had crossed The Channel as a little girl to visit cities like Amsterdam and Paris with her parents, she had never really travelled anywhere. I guess I was just too busy getting on with my life to bother about exploring the big wide world out there, Sarah mused as she watched the flight path mapped out on the screen in front of her. Five hours and eleven minutes till we arrive at our destination, she read. Funny how time just ticks by without asking anyone if it actually suits them. I would have loved to stay longer in England, though. Pity we couldn't meet Karel, but perhaps he and Lucinda will visit us at the end of the year. Still, they don't know what they're letting themselves in for, wanting to come in summer. They'll probably sizzle, but it's the only time they can both make it. Just wait till they see all the kangaroos that hop around the paddocks behind our place! I'll show them around town, the beaches and take them to the café where I used to work. Poor Eric won't be able to take Karel to the football, seeing that the cricket season will have started. I hope North Melbourne do well in the finals, otherwise he'll be miserable for the rest of the year!

Oh, I'm so tired, five hours to go, she yawned. Lucinda's so pretty; if I were a man she would be just my type. Funny how she and Eric had actually met in Brno; it took them long enough to realise it. Imagine if Eric had met her earlier and they had fallen in love… All's well that ends well I guess. The look on Lucinda's face when she discovered that we have the same grandfather! And Irma was so excited to hear that George was alive and doing well perhaps she'll venture out with Lucinda and they can both have a reunion but on second thoughts that may not be such a good idea while my gran is still alive no that wouldn't do but maybe they will sort that one out good old Bedřich we wouldn't have been able to open that safety box without him telling me about his past life and wasn't it exciting going up to London to discover not just the promised jewellery but another diary and that document the secret service were afraid of it all seems so pointless now who really cares what might have happened back then I mean one spy isn't going to topple the government but what do I know in the end and it was so sweet of Irma to let me have one of the garnet-laced necklaces it's so art nouveau-like well it is from the thirties I think I'll wear it to my next exhibition Lucinda was rather keen to read that other diary and I had to act surprised since I knew pretty much most of it from Bedřich but when we continued to read about the role Irma had played in the secret service in the sixties and beyond we were so nonplussed we decided to keep that diary locked up in that safe for a while longer otherwise it would probably get us all into trouble talk about curiosity killing the cat and then discovering Šárka's birth certificate next was the icing on the cake as it meant that Lucinda and I were cousins or second cousins or whatever it's called when you share one grandparent perhaps that's why we got on so well while we were children and even developed the same interests like painting and our tastes in men as I said luckily nothing had developed between her and Eric back in Brno but perhaps the three of us together or maybe I would also fancy Karel you never know but I ought to stop these debauched thoughts or I'll soon start caressing myself oh my now I can't stop yawning and I really liked Lucinda's paintings of the Czech countryside and even her earlier works are marvellous but she just says it's her active compensatory factor as she calls it I know I couldn't live without my art neither psychologically nor financially now thanks to Paolo and his influence in the unpredictably fickle world of art it really rankles when I see what other artists not only get away with but also get praised for but that's just life isn't it perhaps I could recommend Lucinda's work to him and we may even get the chance to exhibit our works together don't know how Eric can just sleep so soundly despite the plane's engines whirring away and the presence of all the other passengers most of whom are glued to their flickering screens God another four and a half hours and Eric was out after only one beer after taking off from Singapore and my thoughts are still uncontrollably racing away shouldn't have drunk that cappuccino at Heathrow Airport perhaps I should also drink some beer as well but then I'll just have to go to the bathroom and probably wake him up in the process I've been up for over twenty hours still awake at this ungodly hour flying over the Indian Ocean somewhere or perhaps we're already hovering over our continent still it'll be good to be back and start painting again I made so many sketches in those cute English villages in Devon oh God am I tired will look a state when we land in the morning but not much worse than most of the other passengers I wonder how they manage to sleep perhaps if I just rest my head on Eric's shoulder he won't even notice just for a little while to relax a bit probably won't work but I'll simply concentrate on his breathing in and out and in and out and in and…